# Looking now at 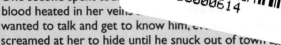 thing different.

One second spent tour... blood heated in her veins... wanted to talk and get to know him, e... screamed at her to hide until he snuck out of town...

He cupped her cheek and ran a thumb over her suddenly dry lips. "Do you really not understand the question?"

"I'm not into big men."

He leaned his forehead against hers. "Do you know how tempting it is to make a tasteless joke right now?"

The laughter bubbled up from her chest. This time she didn't try to stop it. She let the amusement flow through her and wipe out some of the horror of the day.

She gave in to the urge to trail her hand across his chest. Firm dips and bulges pressed against her palm. "You're doing fine."

"That's good, because unless you tell me no, I'm going to kiss you. Long and deep, hot and a bit naughty." He shifted his hands to her hips and pulled her close until his body pressed against hers.

"Jeremy, I—"

"I'll stop before we go too far, because it's been a pretty long and not-so-great day, but believe me when I say I won't want to."

"Still dealing with that surge of adrenalin?"

"Don't give the credit to the danger high. It's been an hour. The night is dark and you're sexy, and if you wiggle like that one more time, I'm throwing you over my shoulder and carrying you into that room." He nodded in the general direction of the door. "And I won't care about my bad timing until tomorrow."

# HELENKAY DIMON

## COPY THAT

HARLEQUIN®
entertain, enrich, inspire™

For Jennifer Dimon—my fabulous niece, the college graduate.
I'm so proud of you!

Recycling programs
for this product may
not exist in your area.

ISBN-13: 978-0-373-69636-9

COPY THAT

Copyright © 2012 by HelenKay Dimon

This edition published by arrangement with Harlequin Books S.A.

For questions and comments about the quality of this book
please contact us at Customer_eCare@Harlequin.ca.

® and TM are trademarks of Harlequin Enterprises Limited or its
corporate affiliates. Trademarks indicated with ® are registered in the
United States Patent and Trademark Office, the Canadian Trade Marks
Office and in other countries.

www.Harlequin.com

**Printed in U.S.A.**

# ABOUT THE AUTHOR

Award-winning author HelenKay Dimon spent twelve years in the most unromantic career ever—divorce lawyer. After dedicating all that effort to helping people terminate relationships, she is thrilled to deal in happy endings and write romance novels for a living. Now her days are filled with gardening, writing, reading and spending time with her family in and around San Diego. HelenKay loves hearing from readers, so stop by her website, www.helenkaydimon.com, and say hello.

## Books by HelenKay Dimon

HARLEQUIN INTRIGUE
1196—UNDER THE GUN*
1214—NIGHT MOVES
1254—GUNS AND THE GIRL NEXT DOOR*
1260—GUNNING FOR TROUBLE*
1297—LOCKED AND LOADED*
1303—THE BIG GUNS*
1352—WHEN SHE WASN'T LOOKING
1369—COPY THAT

*Mystery Men

# CAST OF CHARACTERS

**Jeremy Hill**—The Border Patrol agent is on a work break. He plans to visit his twin brother in sunny San Diego, relax and figure out what happens next in his life. Jeremy never gets to the rest part. When his brother's upstairs neighbor gets attacked and the house blows up, Jeremy realizes his protection days are not over yet.

**Meredith Samms**—She is the girl next door, or in this case, the girl upstairs. She lives a normal life as a kindergarten teacher until Jeremy breaks down the door and everything changes. Through explosions, gunfire and days on the run, she finds an inner strength she didn't know she had, but will she be strong enough to walk away from Jeremy?

**Garrett Hill**—He shares his brother's face and propensity for danger. Someone blew up his house and he wants to know why, but his biggest problem could be winning back the fiancée he left behind.

**Sara Paulson**—Sara sells wedding dresses for a living. She is a hopeless romantic, which is a problem, since her fiancé is clueless and a kidnapper is using her as bait to lure Garrett out.

**Bruce Casden**—Thanks to an undercover operation led by Jeremy, Bruce is in jail and no longer a threat…but no one bothered to tell him that. He has plans. Big plans that include killing the Hill brothers.

**Ellis Martin**—He is Garrett's boss at the Defense Intelligence Agency (DIA). He knows everything about everyone. When Garrett goes missing and Jeremy comes under attack, Ellis steps in. He's the kind of guy who can be trusted with secrets, but he does have a few of his own.

**Andrew Hare**—Ellis's assistant at the DIA has a lot to learn about undercover operations. He's young and a bit green…or is he?

**Joel Kidd**—The newest member of Garrett's team doesn't always follow the rules. He's either the perfect ally or a dangerous mole.

# Chapter One

Meredith Samms heard the front door slam. Not hers. This one belonged to the bottom-floor apartment.

She rented the small one-bedroom tucked into the eaves of the blue craftsman-style house. Her place stretched all of 550 square feet from one end to the other. Still, she paid more per month for the tiny space than her parents paid for a mortgage on a two-story Colonial on an acre in upstate New York. That's what happened when you wanted a piece of what many considered paradise—a home three blocks from the ocean in Coronado, the peninsula of prime real estate across the harbor from downtown San Diego.

Garrett Hill lived in the more spacious apartment downstairs. Not that he stayed there often enough to enjoy it. He traveled most days of the month and had been out of town for three solid weeks. Half the time she knew he was home only when she heard the echo of his heavy footsteps.

This trip struck her as odd, the usual blanket of secrecy lifted. A man she'd never seen before had come to the door two days ago looking for Garrett. A courier had left a package for him, saying Garrett gave her name as someone who could sign for it.

Looked as if he'd broken the whole lone-wolf thing he had going on and she had no idea why. She could ask, even though the chance of getting an answer was slim. Heck, he'd never even told her what he did for a living, and she'd sure poked around that topic several times. Good thing she believed in a healthy dose of persistence.

Slipping off the window seat, she grabbed her key and stuffed it into the back pocket of her cut-off denim shorts. The window air conditioner had lost the race against the unusual scorching July afternoon heat. So much for the theory about San Diego always having perfect seventy-something-degree weather.

Thinking maybe heading downstairs for a visit would keep her T-shirt from sticking to her back, she jogged down the steps, letting her running shoes fall heavily to warn of her impending visit. By the time she hit the small entryway at the bottom of the stairs, she expected Garrett to have his door open. Instead it stayed closed.

She knocked twice. On the second rap, the door slipped open as if the wind had pushed it. Since the air stood deadly still today and Garrett was a bit of a security freak, a ball of anxiety started spinning in her chest. With her past, she didn't scare easily but this scene had Bad Horror Film written all over it.

If she'd lived anywhere other than low-crime, military-presence-everywhere Coronado, she might have bolted. Instead, she eased the door open. "Garrett?"

Only silence bounced back at her.

Her foot crossed the threshold and she heard a small crack. Looking down, she didn't see anything other than sturdy wood painted a bright, shiny white.

When she looked up again, there he was. Not Garrett. Garrett was tall and muscular, but this guy, the non-Garrett, was enormous. Like, size-of-a-truck enormous. He had blond hair and wore all black to match his dark frown.

Alarm bells chimed in her head. She couldn't breathe over the clanking and dinging.

She turned to run, and that fast he was on her. A strong arm wrapped around her waist, trapping her arms against her sides as a hand clamped over her mouth. The oversize dial on his watch dug into her stomach as he spun her around to face the family room again and her feet went airborne. Kicking out as she went, her heel hit the door and slammed it hard against the outside wall.

Despite her defensive efforts, before she could blink she was inside and out of sight of anyone who might walk by. But no way was she giving in without a fight.

She thrashed and shook her head from side to side, hoping for a second where she could ease out of his grip and scream for help. Not that his hand across her mouth stopped her from trying. She yelled until all the air left her lungs, but the sound was muffled against his palm.

Her eyes focused on the room. Her heart rate, which had already kicked to near heart-attack range, tripled its beat. The sofa cushions had long, jagged rips in them. The few photos in the apartment lay on the floor, the glass smashed and scattered among the papers and furniture stuffing.

Seeing the destruction fueled her survival instinct. She kicked, this time hitting bone near his calf and earning a grunt from her attacker. Instead of letting go as planned, his hold over her stomach tightened. Much more of this and he'd strangle her.

She moved her head and opened her mouth, letting him think she intended to scream again. When he adjusted his grip over her lips, she bit down into the meaty part of his palm and didn't stop until she tasted blood.

One second she was standing, nearly bent over from the pressure of his arm against her middle, the next she was spinning through the air. She smacked against the back of the couch with her full weight and felt it bobble and threaten to tip over. One leg folded under her on the cushion as she landed and a shock of pain ran down her spine to her knee.

The combination of dizziness and terror had her stomach heaving. Her vision split in two then refocused just in time to see her attacker looming over her. Blood smeared his cheek and ran down his hand.

"You'll pay for that" was all he said.

The terse phrase was enough to get her moving again, sore knee and all. She scrambled up the back of the couch, clawing her way over shredded cushions and slipping over the top toward the window. Just as one leg hit the floor, he grabbed the other. Two baseball glove–sized hands held her ankle in a viselike grip.

"You're not going anywhere, sweetheart," he said as he started twisting her foot.

She shifted her hips to keep him from breaking it. "What do you want?"

"Came here looking for one thing but looks like I'll be leaving with another." He leered at her as he spoke.

The sick gleam in his dark eyes touched off a frenzy of panic inside her. Her hands shook and the urge to throw up almost overtook her. It had been years since she'd experienced violence. She blocked it so that she could function every day, but the memories kicked to the surface now.

"Please let me go."

The man just laughed. The deep sound, so menacing in its promise of pain, cut across her nerves.

*Keep fighting.* The words flashed in her brain and ran through her, soaking into every pore.

When one of his palms slid up her calf to the back of

her knee, she knew she had a chance. Waiting for just the right moment, when his sick need to control overcame his battle stance, she kicked out as hard as she could. Her heel crashed into his jaw, sending his head flying backward as he yelped in surprise.

She heard the crunch and then she was free. Momentum sent her flying back against the window. She reached for the curtains to steady her weight. With a roaring rip, the rod gave way and she fell on her butt. Wedged between the couch and the wall, she struggled to get her legs under her.

With a rage-filled cry, her attacker reached over the sofa and pulled her to her feet. The bright red cheeks and clenched teeth didn't scare her half as much as the gun in his hand. She had no idea where it had come from, but it was pointed at the center of her chest.

"You'll learn." He practically spit as he talked. His fingers dug into the bare skin of her forearm.

"I have money." She didn't, but she needed time.

The house sat off the main strip filled with tourists and shops, but people walked by all the time on their way to the water. If she could stall long enough, a witness might see her by the window, call the police to check it out.

His gaze crept down the front of her blouse. "You have everything I need right on you."

Disgust clogged her throat as she glanced around looking for something—anything—she could throw through the front window. She spied the overturned lamp on the floor and plotted the best way to drop to the floor and grab it with a man holding on to her arm hard enough to cause bruises.

She'd just resigned herself to a broken arm when she saw a blur of movement behind her attacker. Black hair and stone-cold blue eyes. Six feet of lethal male machine.

Her heart slowed to a jog as the tension rushing through her eased. Everything would be okay now.

Garrett Hill had come home.

The usual military haircut and fatigues were gone, replaced by hair brushed down almost over his eyes and faded blue jeans. In the weeks away, his smile had disappeared but one thing looked the same—his strength. A tight black T-shirt stretched across his wide shoulders and chest, highlighting every muscle.

She'd never been so relieved to see anyone in her life. Her shoulders sagged and she had to fight off a smile when an openmouthed stare replaced the attacker's snarl as Garrett shoved a gun into the back of the other man's head.

"Let the lady go, nice and slow." Garrett reached around and grabbed the other man's gun.

"This isn't over, Hill."

"Sure feels like it is." Garrett nodded his head at her. "Come over here."

She didn't even make it to the other side of the couch before the attacker lunged. He threw his body backward, aiming his head right for Garrett's chin. Garrett shifted in time to deflect the blow, but the attacker turned around. They were face-to-face with the gun trapped between them. Both of their hands held the weapon as Garrett elbowed the other man in the side of the head.

Already injured, the attacker pulled back. Garrett used the opening to wrestle the gun away. It made a short *pffft* sound as he shot the attacker in the knee.

The man went down with a whoosh, squealing and moaning as he dropped to the hardwood. Glass crunched under him where he rolled around.

She watched the blood stream onto the floor right before Garrett slammed his weapon against the attacker's head, sending him into a deadly quiet sprawl.

Then Garrett was there, right in front of her. "Are you okay?"

She tried to look past Garrett's stiff shoulders to the still body below. "Is he dead?"

"Unfortunately, no."

"I don't understand. Who is that?"

"No idea."

"I don't—" The words died in her throat when he touched her shoulder, bringing her gaze back to him. She couldn't remember a time in the year since she'd moved in when he'd touched her. "How can you not recognize him? He was in your house."

"There are two things you need to know." Garrett waited until she nodded before continuing. "First, we need to get out of here right now."

She didn't exactly disagree but she wanted to understand. "Don't we need to…?"

His eyebrow rose. "What?"

"I don't know. Something."

"Okay, then. My second point." He held up another finger. "I'm not Garrett."

# Chapter Two

For the most part, Jeremy Hill thought the woman took both pieces of information pretty well. Didn't balk or ask questions as he steered her to the front door and onto the porch, which was good since he had only a few minutes to get her calm and out of there.

Not many people could face down a trained killer, handle some scary and unexpected information and stay on their feet. Add in a nasty bout of manhandling and she should be screaming by now. But her facial expression didn't even change.

He was impressed.

He had no idea who she was or why she was here. If he had more time, he'd appreciate the sweet pair of legs sticking out from under those shorts. He almost swore when a double kick of attraction and envy hit him. Garrett had kept quiet about this woman. Part of Jeremy understood why.

Of course, Garrett shouldn't be with any woman except his fiancée…or was it former fiancée? Jeremy wasn't sure where that relationship stood, but Garrett's last message had suggested trouble. Not that Jeremy had time to worry about that now.

The woman in front of him started blinking. "Did you hit your head?"

From the look on her face he wondered if *she* had. "Uh, no."

"Fall down?"

He held up both hands, including the one with the loaded gun. "Okay, let me just stop you before you run through every possible injury scenario. I'm fine."

She snorted. "You sure sound like Garrett."

Not the first time he'd heard that. "Probably because I'm his brother."

"Brother?"

"Yes." The confusion hadn't left her eyes, so he nodded to emphasize his answer. "He didn't tell you he had an identical twin?"

Her chest rose and fell on a hard breath. "No, but I guess that would explain it."

"Not a surprise. He tends to be private."

She snorted. "There's an understatement."

Seemed she did know Garrett. In their respective lines of work, the brothers kept their personal lives secret. It was an unspoken way of protecting each other. Their bond could transcend weeks, months even, without communication. They didn't need to announce it in every conversation.

Jeremy had been in the field in Arizona as a Border Patrol agent. He'd come in for a mandatory break. His agenda included nothing more than a few beers and maybe a Padres game. He'd earned some rest and relaxation time. With nothing but miles of desolate desert and days spent chasing drug runners for miles on end, walking into San Diego had been like stepping into a cleansing shower.

Now this. Jeremy didn't know what Garrett had done

or whom he'd ticked off, but something big was happening here and Jeremy had managed to jump right into the middle of it by accident.

So much for the idea of a thirty-day recuperation period while hanging out with his brother by the beach.

Jeremy slipped his cell out of his back pocket and hit a button for the preprogrammed number. He knew the person on the other end would have his identity and location in less than fifteen seconds, with or without the code word. He said it anyway. "Roman five."

The woman in front of him just stared. "What does that—"

"Hill residence." He held up a finger as he talked into the silence on the other end of the phone. Someone somewhere would be taping the distress call and he didn't want her voice being overheard. "Need immediate assistance." He hung up.

She found her first smile; it was shaky but there. "Roman? I'm guessing that's a password?"

He shrugged. "Dramatic but I didn't pick it."

"That was sort of a one-sided conversation."

"All it takes is one call."

"You have a special 'in' with law enforcement the rest of us aren't privy to?"

Clearly the woman had no idea what Garrett did for a living. "My brother has friends in the right places."

"I wouldn't know. He's not exactly the sharing type."

"True. Garrett can keep a secret forever if he needs to." He took his oath seriously. They both did.

Funny how Garrett had even forgotten to mention his pretty neighbor. But Jeremy sure noticed her. Straight shoulder-length blondish-brown hair and big brown eyes. The shirt hinted at a comfortable curviness that trumped the stick-figure California type every time in his book.

He loved the softness of women. Their smell and inviting smiles. Mix that with a wariness of someone who had seen the rougher parts of life and you had his attention.

And how she'd gone after the attacker, waiting for the right moment to strike, was pure magic.

"May as well make this official." He held out his hand. "Jeremy Hill. Younger brother by thirty-four minutes."

She slid her hand into his. "Meredith Samms. Kindergarten teacher and woman right on the edge of vomiting."

"Please don't. I'd honestly rather you shoot me." He'd take a firefight over dry heaving any day.

"Believe it or not, I'm trying not to be sick."

Way he figured it, help was still two minutes away. He'd hoped to take her mind off the horror then get her down the steps and out without incident, but his time was up. They had to go.

"You teach your students those kicking moves?"

"I might now." She inhaled and let her breath out nice and slow as she stared at a fixed point across the street. "I like to think I'm pretty smart, but I'm totally confused about what's going on here."

"Understandable."

"My hands won't stop shaking." She turned her palms up.

He slid his hands under hers and felt her nerves jump around. When he realized his did, too, and not from fear, he dropped his arms to his sides. "Adrenaline. It will pass."

"Will the urge to throw up?"

He sure hoped so. "That takes a bit more practice."

He glanced through the window into the ransacked family room, seeing if there was anything he could salvage before they booked out of there. Guy still knocked out on the floor. *Good.* Nothing else looked much like it was worth keeping. Jeremy knew without a full house inspection the only thing that mattered, or had any value, stood in front of him with eyes the size of basketballs.

"Anyone else in the house, to your knowledge?" he asked as he eased away from the door and down the stairs, taking her with him toward the sidewalk without even touching her.

"No." She rubbed her hands up and down her arms as she took turns peeking at the door and watching her step.

"You haven't seen Sara?"

Meredith stopped moving. "Who's Sara?"

Well, that answered the question about the current state of Garrett's love life. "That sounds like a 'no' on Sara."

The questions kept piling up. Jeremy planned to track down his brother the second they got out of there and start asking a few.

"I thought Garrett was home, but I guess not," Meredith said.

"Just me, and I walked in on that guy. Watched him for about fifteen minutes to see what he was looking for." Jeremy cleared his throat as he tried to block the guilt kicking his gut. "I'm sorry I didn't get to you sooner. I had a problem by the back door and had to find a way around it."

"I'm fine." Meredith shook her head, as if trying to block out his words. "Are the police on the way?"

"I hope not."

She finally landed on the last step. "Excuse me?"

"We don't need them."

She backed away. The move wasn't huge, more like inches, but she shifted into a clear path for a run down the front walk to the street. "Now I'm really confused."

Jeremy chose his words carefully. No need to spook her even more. With his luck today, she'd panic and accidentally jump in front of a car. "We need a certain level of expertise here."

"I don't know what that means." Her words came out slow and measured.

Yeah, she was right on the edge of bolting. He could see it in every line of her body and in the tension stretching across her lips.

"Remember how it took me a few extra minutes to get to you and how I told you we had to get out of the house as fast as possible?"

"Uh-huh."

"Here's the other thing I said was important." He hesitated until her face paled. "It's under control now, but—"

"Jeremy, just tell me."

"The back door is rigged with explosives."

A NEW WAVE of panic crashed over Meredith. Her knees buckled and she would have gone right down except for the sudden touch of Jeremy's hands under her elbows.

"Whoa." He ducked his head until his gaze met hers. "You okay?"

"We have to get out of here." She looked up and down the street, her movements frantic and out of control now, every cell in her body exploding into action. "Clear the neighborhood so no one gets hurt."

"It's fine."

She dug her fingernails into the bare skin of his forearms. "How can you say that?"

"The trigger is hooked to the door. Well, was. I detached it."

"So it's safe."

"I'm not an explosives expert, but it can't blow unless someone rigs it again." He let go of her and grabbed keys out of his front jeans pocket. "You're going to get in my car and drive away from here—"

"But you said—"

"Just as a precaution." He held up his hands as if surrendering to her. "And I'm going to wait for the team to arrive."

She could barely hear him over the buzzing in her ears. "What team?"

"Garrett's people." Jeremy put the keys in her palm and closed her fingers over them.

Her mind spun and the first stupid thought in her head ran right to her mouth. "I don't have my wallet or my license."

The corner of Jeremy's mouth kicked up in a smile but his eyes stayed steely cold. "Not your biggest problem at the moment."

"I guess not." Reality settled over her. "Tell me the truth. Are you staying calm so I don't panic?"

His mouth opened and closed before answering. "Yes."

"But this is bad, right?"

"Very."

For some reason, the honesty eased the spinning ball of terror inside her. "Okay. This doesn't have anything to do with the package, right?"

"I don't know what you're talking about."

"Someone dropped off a package for Garrett. It was wrapped in brown paper and this big." She made a square with her hands. "It stuck with me because it was so odd. Maybe that's what the guy was looking for."

"I think he wanted Garrett."

She had no idea what to say to that. "Oh."

"I'll do a quick check." Jeremy put his hand on the small of her back and edged her in the direction of the car. "It's the blue Mustang. You go."

She looked over her shoulder, about to make a comment on his car choice being the same as Garrett's except in color, when she saw a flash in the front-door window.

Jeremy took one look at her expression and his face went blank. He spun around and raced up the porch steps. He yanked the door open then slammed it shut just as fast.

Before she could blink, he shot back down the steps, his feet barely touching as he reached for her. His hands landed on her shoulders as he half pushed, half shoved her toward the street.

Her sneakers skidded across the sidewalk at the end of the small front yard before a surge of hot air swept underneath her body, sending it airborne. Her muscles went weightless as a clap of thunder exploded behind her.

As she flew, the air stopped as if sucked up into a vacuum, then rolled back out in a rush. Burning heat licked at her from every direction. Her skin itched, feeling all prickly and singed, but all she could see was the ground rushing up to meet her face.

She would have crashed headfirst into the street but Jeremy twisted, his arms coming around her, as his back knocked against the hard cement and she slammed into his chest. Their bodies bounced and her vision blurred, then focused long enough for her to see him grimace.

With his face right next to hers, she heard his sharp inhale over what sounded like a thundering drumroll. She struggled to sit up, but he dragged her back down, pulling her under him and covering every inch of her body with his. He probably outweighed her by a good seventy pounds, and the added heat from his skin nearly suffocated her.

She peeked through the small space between his arm and the ground and saw shoes and the tires of a car stopped in the middle of the street. When she swallowed, her ears popped and the muffled echoes gave way to screaming reality. She could hear sirens and talking and someone calling her name.

Jeremy lifted his body off hers and tugged on her shoulder until she flipped to her back. The burning smell hit her, like the scent of fireplaces during the few cold days of the year, but that couldn't be right. It was summer.

"Meredith, open your eyes."

The command came to her in a raspy voice and she obeyed without thinking. A man loomed over her, his face dark with soot and eyes filled with concern. It took her a second to put the pieces together. "Jeremy?"

He nodded. "Are you okay?"

"I'm not sure." She struggled to sit up.

He turned to talk to a group of people gathered around them. "Everybody step back."

She could hear questions and bits of conversation all around her. And the crackling—it was as if someone was breaking bunches of twigs right next to her ear.

This time she grabbed on to Jeremy's muscled arms and used him to help her crawl off the ground. He sat back on his heels, taking her with him to a sitting position.

Her heart sputtered to a stop as she sat on the sidewalk and watched the flames devour her house. The lower floor was nothing more than a mass of bright red and orange. Sparks rose into the air as the fire tore through the trees, walls, furniture—all gone.

Glass covered the grass. Upstairs, the only thing she recognized was the tattered remains of her once pretty off-white eyelet curtain blowing through the opening of what remained of her bedroom window.

"It's just stuff," he whispered, but his voice rose above the sirens, squealing tires and the older woman who stood in the street and wailed in horror about "the dev-il's heat"...whatever that meant.

Through it all Meredith felt the heat of Jeremy's stare and finally faced him. "I'm fine."

"You sure?" He glanced down to where she had his shirt in a stranglehold.

"Sorry." She forced her fingers to unclench.

"No problem."

"Everything is gone." She didn't know she'd said the words out loud until Jeremy grunted. She looked at him again, watching him scan the crowd. Tension radiated off him as every muscle pulled taut. "Are you okay?"

"We need to get out of here." He glanced at a point over her shoulder and gave a small nod.

"What are you—"

He stood, stopping about halfway up as his lips turned white and he swore.

"Jeremy." Seeing him in pain, she jumped to her feet and slipped her shoulder under his arm to help him the rest of the way up. "You're hurt."

"I'll be fine," he said through clenched teeth, as he signaled to someone behind her. "At least we know what was probably in that mystery package."

"A bomb."

"I saw a guy hold up a cell phone, likely a secondary trigger, right before I bolted down the steps."

Her mind rebelled. Rather than dealing with what he was saying, she shifted to nurse mode. "You need medical attention."

"Later. We're leaving."

"Where are we going?" She struggled under his weight. "And please say 'to the hospital.'"

"Somewhere safe."

When the black SUV stopped in front of them and the back door opened, she wondered if his idea of safe looked anything like hers.

## Chapter Three

The driver opened the door and slid out of his seat. Gravel crunched under his shoes as he walked the four steps to the sidewalk. The fire crackled around them and more people gathered as the wailing sirens drew closer.

The man lowered his sunglasses but gave the flames little more than a quick glance. His unblinking attention focused on Jeremy as his eyes narrowed. "Garrett?"

Through a haze of pain, radiating from his side and screaming through every cell, Jeremy conducted a visual check of his own. He detected two weapons under slight bulges and assumed there were at least twice as many hidden beneath the other man's out-of-place black jacket and dark jeans.

The combination of the heat, fire and heavy clothing would melt most guys in a matter of seconds. Not this one. Not a drop of sweat on him. The cool cockiness almost convinced Jeremy without verification that this was one of Garrett's men. Almost.

"I'm his brother." Jeremy left his badge in his back pocket, since his face made his connection to Garrett clear. "You?"

"We need to leave."

"No way am I getting in that car," Meredith whispered under her breath as she inched her way to Jeremy's far side.

He understood. Smart women stayed on constant guard. They didn't trust men they didn't know and they certainly didn't get into cars with two strangers. He appreciated the fear, even admired her smarts, but she still didn't have a choice. Until he knew what was going on and who had launched the attack, he planned to stay close.

First, he had to confirm the identity of their driver. Danger pulsed all around them without adding more.

"Westfield 78." The man said the prearranged security code.

The tension strangling Jeremy's shoulders eased. "Durham 72."

"Excuse me?" She looked from one man to the other. "Are we just saying random words?"

Jeremy fought off a smile for the first time since this whole mess started. "An old high-school basketball score."

Her eyes bulged. "Is now the time for that?"

The man nodded. "Joel Kidd."

Jeremy knew the name. Garrett never talked about his operations, only the team he'd handpicked and admired. His success depended on being surrounded by loyal men who could fight, then blend into their surroundings for a quick getaway.

Joel glanced in the direction where the house had once stood. "Tell me Garrett's not in there."

"He isn't." Jeremy inhaled long and deep in an effort to bring his heartbeat out of thumping range and focus his thoughts.

"Hostiles?"

"Two in the house. One definitely went out in a ball of fire because he was unconscious. Unconfirmed on the other. Could be more on the scene."

A fire truck raced around the end of the block and headed right for them. As it sped up, Joel's detachment faded. "Authorities are here, which means questions. We need to leave."

Meredith frowned. "If by 'authorities' you mean police, then no. They're the good guys." When neither man said anything, Meredith's frown deepened. "Right?"

Joel opened the back door. "Get in."

Meredith pivoted, her body facing away from him as if ready for flight. "Not to sound like I have trust issues, but no."

"You know me." Jeremy waved Joel off when his hand shifted to his hip. Jeremy knew what that meant. "It's safe."

One nod or an eyebrow lift and Joel would render her unconscious. Jeremy preferred to have her permission for this trip. It would make whatever came next much easier if she trusted him. He also hated the idea of taking a woman out even if it qualified as the safest way of extracting a potential victim.

"I know your brother, not you. And it would appear I barely know him." She sneaked her third peek at the police car stopping a house away.

"Same thing."

"Not quite."

Joel shoved his glasses back on his nose and dropped his hands to his sides. "I can put her in the car."

She whipped around to face him. "What does that mean?"

"Nothing good." Which was why Jeremy refused to use that option.

She inched her feet back, edging closer to the people gathered behind them. "You're not making me feel more confident."

"Until I know what's happening here, I want you protected," Jeremy said as he continued to scan the area for easy exits and potential threats.

She nodded. "The police are right over—"

"Protected by me. Garrett would kill me if I did otherwise." Jeremy put his hand on her elbow before she could bolt. He pulled her toward the car in a tug he hoped appeared to bystanders as more concerned and loving than covert. "And we need to go now."

She shifted her weight to her heels and skidded to a stop. "Are you running from the police or something?"

"I'm a different kind of law enforcement. Border Patrol. And I'm trying to get us out of here before the guy who set off the explosion finds us."

Her body went limp at that. "You think the guy from the front door is still alive?"

"I'm not willing to wait around and find out." Jeremy took advantage of her momentary shock and crowded her against the side of the car.

His body blocked her view of the house and, more importantly, the police's view of her. Using his weight and height advantage, he pressed against her until she lifted her leg and slipped onto the seat.

Joel's mouth kicked up. "Nice move." He jumped into the driver's seat.

Without Joel's shoulders blocking the view, Jeremy saw the other end of the street. Spied the man standing behind a trio of neighborhood wives who were still holding a bottle of wine and glasses as they hovered in a yard three houses down. It was the same man who'd triggered the blaze.

The roar of the car engine as it turned over bolted Jeremy into action. "Hold up."

"I never agreed…" She followed Jeremy's gaze, peeking over the seat in front of her. "What's wrong with you? What do you see?"

"The bomber." Jeremy already had the door open and his feet on the ground.

She grabbed his sleeve. She weighed all of 130 pounds and she trapped his elbow in a deadlock. "Don't you dare leave this car."

"He's headed between two houses near the end of the street."

"And you are not leaving me alone—" her gaze flicked to the back of Joel's head "—here."

Joel eyed her in the rearview mirror. "I won't hurt you."

The churning in Jeremy's gut revved up when the bomber ducked behind the house.

This time she dug her fingernails into his arm. "Yeah, well, I've seen enough woman-abducted-and-left-in-pieces-in-a-box television specials not to take your word for it."

Jeremy knew he could rip his arm out of her grasp, but he didn't want to hurt her. Didn't want to lose his one lead either. "Not sure what to say to that, but—"

Her second hand joined the first and she started tugging him back into the car as he looked around. "No."

One of the policemen herding the crowds onto the sidewalk picked that moment to look up. His gaze zeroed in on the SUV and Jeremy knew his time for an explosive run had passed. Scram now and he'd have the police following.

Jeremy ground his teeth together. "The guy is getting away."

"You're the one who insisted on dragging me along with you, so now you're stuck."

Joel barked out a laugh. "Guess she told you."

Jeremy took one last look at the policeman. He waved off the woman talking to him and reached for the radio on his shoulder. Jeremy knew the drill. The officer would run Joel's license plates. Then who knew what would happen.

"This car yours?" Jeremy asked as he closed the door again and leaned back in his seat. He winced over the ripping sensation in his side but pushed the pain out of his mind.

"It's registered to a company."

"A real one?"

"On paper only."

Meredith surrendered the death grip on his arm but didn't let go. "That's comforting."

Despite his fury over losing his prey, Jeremy agreed with her sarcasm. "Drive around the corner and I'll see if I can find our guy on the next block."

"You're still not leaving this car." She mumbled the comment as she stared at his profile.

Jeremy tried to remember the last time he'd let a woman's begging derail a chase. Then it hit him…never.

ELLIS MARTIN SMOOTHED his fingers over his mustache. He'd had the thing for almost thirty years, since he graduated from college. The small action soothed him. In this case, it kept him from exploding all over his new and supposedly brilliant assistant.

His throat ached with the need to scream, but Ellis fought back the rage. "I've run out of patience."

"I understand, sir. But—"

"Stop there." All the impressive grades in his Ivy League education hadn't taught Andrew Hare the common-sense business principle of knowing when to shut up and listen. Ellis decided the younger man had better learn quickly or he'd have one of the shortest tenures in the Defense Intelligence Agency ever—four days.

Counterintelligence demanded a steep learning curve, and so far Andrew had spent most of his time repeating instructions. Book smart, maybe. Capable of reading reactions and completing difficult tasks? Not so far.

"Excuse me, sir?"

And he said *excuse me* far too often. "Hill has been out of contact and running for a week now. I've had enough. You bring Hill back here, now. In pieces if you have to."

"We have a problem."

"That's not a sentence I want to hear." Ellis leaned back in his big leather chair. He wrapped his fingers around the arms to fight off the urge to strangle Andrew. Human Resources hated that sort of thing.

"I know, but—"

His nails dug a little deeper. "I want results, not excuses."

"Our man just got to the scene. He says the place is on fire."

"What?"

"Witnesses said they heard a loud bang. An explosion. The windows blew out and the fire raced out of control almost immediately." Andrew talked so fast the sentences ran into each other.

Ellis glanced over his shoulder. If his office had a window, if any of the offices on this floor had one, it would be right behind him. Instead, this part of the suite consisted of interior rooms. No one could look in, and thanks to a list of security procedures, no information got out. Or that was the theory.

"It was a gas leak." He'd said the response enough times for it to become automatic. The cover worked well enough for him to have the appropriate form in his desk and an electric-company official on speed dial.

"How can you know that?" Andrew asked.

Ellis wondered if the idea of on-the-job training was such a good idea after all. From now on he'd insist on hiring the guy with street smarts and a B average over the one with the shiny résumé that appealed to a hiring committee worried about recruiting the best on-paper students available.

"Within a week we will discover the cause. It will be a gas leak. I can guarantee it."

"I see."

Ellis seriously doubted that. "Where's Hill now?"

"Gone."

With the news of the explosion, Ellis had started analyzing his options, but all of that slammed to a halt with this latest development. Every breath of air sucked out of the room until the dark-paneled room closed in like a prison cell. "Hill went up with the house?"

"I don't..."

Ellis stood up, every muscle in his body snapping to life. "Either say what you need to say right now or I'll transfer you to a field office in Alaska and find someone else to do your job."

Andrew cleared his throat. When he spoke again, gone was the nervous newbie who shook enough to rattle his teeth when he talked. This time his voice rang clear and deep as his shoulders pulled tight into military attention. "Our guy on the ground is hearing reports about Hill getting away."

"How?"

"In a car. He had help."

"Who?"

"Unclear at the moment." Andrew gave his report and

checked his notes, suddenly acting like a seasoned pro. "Someone who drives a car registered to Foxtrot Enterprises."

Ellis didn't need to look up the name. Hill had created the corporate entity as part of his cover. Ellis paid the monthly lease on the car every month from the budget for Hill's team.

"So, inside help." An internal debate waged in Ellis as to whether that was a good or bad thing. Garrett alone was lethal. Operating with his dedicated team made him unstoppable.

"It would appear so, sir."

"Keep in mind nothing is ever as it appears with Garrett Hill. We trained him to defy expectations, so confirm every detail before you take it as gospel."

"I'll see what I can find out."

"You have an hour."

## Chapter Four

When the car eased around the corner and slowed to a stop, Meredith thought she'd gone to sleep and woken up in the middle of a strange action movie. She leaned forward, balancing her elbows on her knees. Her hands shook as she examined the cuts and scrapes on her palms.

Real people went to the hospital after being thrown by an explosion and nearly turned into a piece of burned toast. Real people did not chase after bad guys. Real people ran to the police and screamed for help.

Real life sure didn't include finding out about a previously unknown twin brother or hanging out with men who carried guns. Not her life. Not anymore. She'd left violence behind in favor of stability. She didn't run from the law.

She glanced over and saw the gun in Jeremy's hand. Heard him tap his foot against the floor as his knee bounced to the steady rhythm only he could hear. "Who are you?"

His focus never wavered. He stared out the window. "Jeremy Hill."

"You know what I mean."

His gaze locked on her, all his intensity boring into her, and the next words she intended to say jammed in her throat.

"I'm going to protect you."

The promises men made. "I've heard that before."

At nineteen she'd heard and believed them. Vows of love and fidelity, talk of being together forever. But between the sweet touches and mind-blowing kisses he'd drop a line about her weight. About her friends being loud or dumb. About her leaving school and following him back to the Midwest because she wouldn't need a job once they settled in their house.

She justified his behavior and made excuses for the way he isolated her. The latter made her nuts. She sneaked out to meet friends for coffee and ignored their concerned stares and dropped comments about male friends they knew who would love her. She pretended she didn't hear the whispers as she walked away and fell deeper into his cocoon of supposed protection.

Just thinking about those days made her stomach tumble until she thought it would roll right out of her and land on the floor. The familiar fear rushed back and momentarily panicked her. The bile in her throat and trembling in her muscles—it all played like a broken record of a song she'd rather forget.

Clint had stolen something from her and she'd been fighting her entire adult life to get it back. Dignity. Self-respect.

The safety classes and hours logged at the shooting range helped. But now, sitting in a car with men she didn't know, all those old insecurities rushed over her. She fought off waves of debilitating self-bashing and reached for that inner balance she'd vowed never to lose again.

Jeremy's eyes narrowed. "What does that cryptic comment mean?"

"I don't need a man to take care of me."

"This isn't a liberation issue or some sort of battle of the sexes."

"Really? Feels like it."

"No one appreciates a strong woman more than I do. I saw you kick and fight and go after that intruder. You're a survivor and there's nothing more attractive to me than that."

Joel cleared his throat. "Uh, Jeremy? Maybe we should focus."

Jeremy talked over him. The rise in his voice's volume was the only nod to the fact that Joel had made any noise. "But, like it or not, we have to be realistic about men's physical advantages. Weight and strength all matter. I'm not saying you can't win, but it's not easy."

She didn't want size to play a role, but she was smart enough to know it did. Her self-defense instructor made that clear. He also gave some hints on how to even the battle.

"I'm quite familiar with men who lead with fists," she said.

Jeremy's gaze wandered over her face. It felt as if an hour passed before he spoke again, though it was probably more like seconds. "I don't want the guy hunting for Garrett to target you. He'll have a gun—"

"I can shoot."

Jeremy's head snapped back as if he hadn't expected that answer. He glanced at Joel in the mirror then back to her. "Practicing on a target or cans of whatever and actually aiming at a person are different things."

She knew that all too well, but she had no intention of sharing that information. "And?"

"I'll shoot without blinking."

"People will look for me. I have friends and neighbors. People are going to ask questions."

At least, she hoped that was true. She hadn't lived in Coronado long. She spent her time reading in the park and dreaded any invitation to hang out in a bar with co-workers looking for men. The whole "get drunk and find some random guy to sleep with" thing left her feeling hollow. She wasn't a prude but the bar scene, complete with all the stupid games and fake attraction stunts, had never appealed to her.

Joel stretched his arm along the back of the seat. "She's right. Her absence will cause questions."

"I'm only asking for a few hours." Jeremy's jaw tightened to the point of cracking with each word. "You can trust me that long."

"Not if you're running around shooting at people."

"Last time I pulled a weapon I stopped a guy from touching you."

The memories of the horrible morning bombarded her. The headache kicked in a second later. "True."

"Sorry." He exhaled as he put his hand on her knee. "Look, someone tried to kill my brother, to kill you. I need to know who and why so I can protect you both. And time is slipping away. The guy has a huge head start. It may already be too late to find a trail."

"Good." The answer worked for both his comment and for the warmth spiraling through her body at the touch of his palm against her bare skin.

"I'll be careful, but I do need to do this." He gave her leg a quick squeeze then tapped on the back of Joel's seat. "Stay here."

She was no longer panicked about her safety. Now she was ticked off. Being dragged around without any explanation did that to a woman.

"Absolutely not," she said in her best teacher voice.

The locks clicked right before Joel turned around. "For the record, I agree with the lady."

"My name is Meredith."

"Meredith." He smiled at her before his mouth flatlined and his attention returned to Jeremy. "How does this play out? There are cops everywhere. We have a civilian in the car."

*Civilian?*

"Unlock the door." Jeremy's deep voice rattled with a deadly echo.

A second click bounced around the silent car. Then he was gone.

The whole rescuer thing should impress her. In some ways it did. In others it filled her with flaming frustration. If Jeremy intended to save her, she needed him to be alive to do it.

"Let's go." She opened the door before Joel could lock her in. That would teach him to hesitate.

"Whoa." He jumped out of the car and raced around to meet her at the hood.

"That's the fastest I've seen you move since you drove up."

"I'll be running pretty damn fast when Jeremy tries to kill me for letting you out of this car."

"I'm not rushing in to help. You are."

"Wait, what?"

The plan seemed simple enough in her head, but Joel's scowl suggested otherwise. "I know you won't leave me alone. I also know Jeremy should have backup. So, you move and I hang back and then maybe, just maybe, we'll live through the next ten minutes."

"I can't guarantee that."

"Or I can scream for the police and end this now."

His entire demeanor changed. His hand went to his

gun and he rolled his shoulders back as every inch of him vibrated with a new alertness. "You don't fight fair."

She doubted he even knew how. With the mention of a battle he automatically prepared to step in. That instinct appeared to be ingrained. "I have a feeling it might be the only way to win an argument with you or Jeremy."

JEREMY TRIED TO concentrate on tracking but Meredith's comments ran through his head. He'd seen her survival instinct in action. He'd expected her to shake and cry after being pawed and nearly blown up. Any sane person would. Instead, she'd soldiered through.

Now she talked about guns and protection like a woman who had done battle and knew there were rarely any real winners when it came to violence. Made him wonder what she'd seen in her life and who had taught her those tough lessons.

The idea of her being on the receiving end made him want to hit someone. He still wanted to kick his own butt for not being able to disarm the device at the back door and get to her faster when that animal touched her in Garrett's family room.

In a little over an hour she'd managed to worm her way into his thoughts. Instead of focusing on the task in front of him, he was thinking about her past.

It wasn't the first time that worrying about a woman had thrown him off stride. He had the knife wound in his side as a constant reminder.

He stopped along the side of a house. Without moving, he drew on his powers of concentration, trying to bring his focus back to the hunt. He shoved out the sirens and talking, the roar of the fire and chatter from all the people gathered to watch Garrett's house melt into ash.

Centered again, Jeremy slipped into the backyard of

the beige bungalow at the end of the block. He took in the small patch of grass and the fenced-in vegetable garden in the far left corner. Two steps led up to an entrance and an open screen door. No one lingered, but the attacker could have dragged a new victim into the house as his shield.

The tingle at the base of his neck had Jeremy glancing behind him. The sight of Joel sneaking across the lawn and Meredith hovering within shooting range sent rage burning through him. He didn't need a team. He'd planned to go in and out before Meredith faced one more second of danger.

Not going to happen now.

At the near-silent tap of a shoe against cement, Jeremy tensed, waiting for the shot to come. He ducked as he spun around, but the attacker made his move and launched his body off the top step at Jeremy's midsection.

The flash of a gun and a hint of a feral smile. A heavy body crashed into Jeremy, slamming him into the flagstone path leading around the house and sending his gun skidding into the grass. Air rushed out of his lungs as his side screamed with blinding pain.

In the second before his vision cleared and his senses returned, his attacker pinned his arm to the ground with his knee. Jeremy's muscle cramped and tore as he tried to roll the other man off him. He shifted enough to nail the guy in the back with his leg.

Jeremy could hear Joel's shouts and Meredith's cries for help. Knowing they were closing in and drawing unwanted attention, that with one simple shift the attacker could shoot and take them out, Jeremy dipped into his strength reserves. He bucked his hips and grabbed for the gun in the grass as he knocked his other fist into the side of his attacker's head.

"Put the weapon down!" Joel yelled.

Footsteps slapped against the walkway as Joel and Meredith came closer. Jeremy grabbed for the attacker's gun. Anything to keep it from pointing in Meredith's direction. Joel could fight back and defend. He had the training and the skills. She was an innocent bystander.

Jeremy's fingers wrapped around the hot metal as he strained to push the barrel toward the other man. Jeremy braced his back against the ground as he kicked out to unbalance his attacker. The guy's quick look at Joel gave Jeremy an opening. He slammed his elbow into the attacker's jaw, sending his head flying back and loosening his hold on the gun.

Jeremy tore the weapon away, ready to fire, but the attacker stopped him with a sucker punch, right on his fresh wound.

Fire raced through Jeremy's body as his breath hiccuped and his body jackknifed. Pain exploded in every brain cell. His fingers went numb and the gun dropped to the ground next to him.

With a sound somewhere between a roar and a laugh, the attacker slipped a knife out of his belt and aimed it right for Jeremy's gut. One second he saw the other man's teeth and a face splotched red with rage. The next a boom thundered around them.

As if in slow motion, the attacker slid off Jeremy and fell to his side. Blood trickled from the small hole in his forehead as a sea of red pooled beneath him in the grass.

Jeremy looked up in time to see the bleak determination in Joel's eyes as he lowered his weapon. He'd done exactly what Garrett had taught him to do…kill the bad guys. The question was whether the answers they needed stopped with the man bleeding out on the ground.

"Jeremy!"

"I'm okay." He could barely move his mouth, but he

forced the words out. He also put up a hand to keep Meredith from plowing into him as part of her rescue plan.

A few more seconds and he'd pass out. Being knocked unconscious would be the perfect ending to this crappy day. But instead of hugging him, she dropped to her knees and brushed her hands over his chest as if he were made of glass.

"He shot you."

"How did that happen?" Joel checked the attacker for a pulse then took up position on Jeremy's other side.

"It didn't." Jeremy leaned on both of them to sit up and couldn't hide the sharp inhale when he pressed his hand against his side. "He alive?"

"No," Joel said.

"There's blood all over you." She reached over Jeremy to Joel. "Give me your jacket."

Joel didn't hesitate. He ripped it off his shoulders and wadded it into a ball.

When she pressed it against the wound, Jeremy's world started to spin. "Not shot."

Meredith bunched his shirt in her fist and exposed his bare chest before returning the makeshift bandage to his side. "He got you."

"Old knife wound. I reopened it. Not a big deal." With each breath he took, the house in front of him shimmered and shifted. With his head tilted to the side, the landscape morphed from bright colors to dull gray. That had to be a bad sign.

"That's it. No more excuses." She jumped to her feet but stayed crouched at his side. "We need to get you to a hospital."

Jeremy grabbed her arm and tightened until the black-and-white vision in front of him blurred then shifted back into place.

"She's right." Joel took out his cell. "You need medical attention."

"Just a safe house and a first-aid kit." Jeremy tried to harness all his energy to get to his feet. If he sprawled on his back he'd lose any chance of convincing them to go along with his plan.

"You'll bleed to death if we don't get you help." She nodded at her hand and the blood seeping through the jacket.

She had a point but he wasn't ready to admit it. "I need an ID on the dead guy and for someone to find Garrett."

Jeremy pushed out the worst fears about his brother being hurt or injured. He'd know. He'd feel it in his gut. The connection they shared extended that far. It bound them when the miles kept them apart for months. Like when Garrett got shot two years ago and lay bleeding in a hospital in a country where no one knew his name. Jeremy had sensed it all.

"You win. I'll call it in to the office." Joel pressed a few buttons, then put the cell to his ear.

All the color rushed out of her cheeks. "You two can't be serious about treating this with simple first aid."

"We're going into hiding," Jeremy said.

Her hands flattened against his chest. "We?"

"The two of us."

"Oh, really?" Her voice turned positively frosty as she sat back on her heels.

For some reason, her slip from panic to angry teacher mode restored some of his strength. "I'm afraid you're going to be stuck with me for a while longer."

"Who says?"

That one was easy. "Me."

## Chapter Five

"It's been an hour and thirteen minutes since you went to collect information. I've been paging you for the last ten." Ellis stopped pacing and shuffling the papers in his hands long enough to glare at Andrew. "You'd better have some good news to explain your delay."

"Not exactly." Andrew shut the office door behind him and stepped inside. Not far. Just in front of the door at the edge of the dark blue carpet. As if distance would save him from his new boss's wrath.

"And by that do you mean 'no'?"

"Garrett Hill is still missing." The younger man visibly swallowed but his voice stayed strong. He didn't as much as shift his feet as he delivered the bad news.

"Unacceptable."

Andrew spent far too long studying the file in front of him before responding. "Our man in Coronado says—"

"Stop." Ellis dropped his stack of folders on the desk and slid into his chair. The silence stretched out, ratcheting up the tension as it built. He could have eased the choking panic in the room, but he fed off it instead, letting the quiet throw the younger man further off balance.

"Sir?"

"I don't care what anyone says."

"Excuse me?"

"Call the operative back in. While you're at it, tell him to bring his government passport and security badge with him, because if he can't track a man escaping a fire in the middle of broad daylight he's done at this agency." So much for sending the guy with a decade of service to cover his top man. Garrett Hill could slip any tail. That's what made him so good.

"But according to our guy there was a pretty big crowd around the fire. It would have been easy for anyone to move in or out of there without being noticed."

Ellis flipped a switch on his desk and a bank of monitors to the left flickered to life. "There are people in this office who get paid to keep me updated on what's happening everywhere in the world. I need you to establish other skills if you want to remain useful."

He also had a file on his desk filled with photos and status reports and backgrounds on every person in Garrett's neighborhood. Ellis had possession of redacted top secret reports on the brother and a separate paper consisting of less than a paragraph about some woman named Meredith Samms, a woman Garrett should have run through a background check before allowing her to move into his house.

When Ellis debriefed Garrett he'd add in a question or two about that. Being the best didn't mean he could ignore the rules. Well, not all of them.

Ellis glanced up and noticed Andrew hadn't moved an inch in five minutes. *Good.*

Now, on to the next issue. "Locate Darren Mitchell."

"Right now?"

"Yes, Andrew."

"But he's no longer with the DIA."

"It would appear we're back to the obvious."

Andrew's eyebrow rose and an uncharacteristic spark of anger flashed in his eyes. "Excuse me?"

Ellis took the show of emotion as a good sign. He admired people who stood their ground. The weak wasted his time. "I'm aware of Darren's work status with this agency, since I'm the one who fired him after Garrett filed his last operation report."

"My point is that we can no longer track the man through the building or in his car or at his house by using his badge or the GPS tags."

"There are other ways. He's wearing an ankle monitor. It was one of the conditions of his bail. Get me a report on where he's been and with whom. Also check the video surveillance."

"Excuse me?"

"Say that again and you're fired." Satisfaction flowed through him when Andrew's mouth snapped shut. "We're tracking Darren's moves."

"All the time?"

"Yes. We used the Federal Intelligence Surveillance Act and got a warrant. We know everything he says and does, or we should. Your job is to check for loopholes."

"Anyone else?"

"Garrett Hill has many enemies, the most immediate and obvious one being the fellow agent he turned in for extortion. With Darren's trial looming, he is a logical choice for investigation. He takes out Garrett, he stands a better chance of walking away clean."

MEREDITH PULLED BACK the thin yellow curtain with the strange flower print and stared out at the empty motel parking lot. The SUV they'd driven here had disappeared. Except for Joel walking back and forth in front of the door as he talked on the phone, there wasn't any sign of life out there. Just the sun bouncing off the black pavement as it dipped lower on the horizon.

They'd driven across the bridge into downtown San Diego and kept heading east until the neighborhoods disappeared and nothing stood in front of them except a row of mountains. She had no idea where they were or how long they'd been in the car. She'd been too focused on keeping pressure on Jeremy's stomach. Every flat, muscled inch of it.

"It's not exactly four-star accommodations." Despite the slight slur around the edges of his voice, it boomed strong and deep through the small room with the queen-size bed and bright orange bedspread.

She let the curtain drop and moved back to the bed. The white bandage glowed against his tan skin. She'd cleaned the wound then watched and winced as Joel stitched Jeremy up. Through it all, he gritted his teeth and introduced her to some inventive swearing combinations, but he never said anything else. Never yelled. It was as if he were made of steel.

She sat down next to him, careful not to let the bed dip or the shake of the cheap mattress jostle him. "I've stayed in worse."

He curled one arm under his head and propped his body up on the flat pillows. "You need to date guys who treat you better."

"I was paying my own way at the time."

"I know you and Garrett…that you guys are…" Jeremy stared at the ceiling, his gaze following the lines in the crisscross panel design. "It's not my business, but maybe he said something to you during some of your private time together. Something that didn't seem important at the time."

"I was his tenant."

Jeremy's gaze shot back to hers. Bright blue eyes held her fixed in place. "Tenant?"

"I rented the upstairs apartment."

He shook his head then closed his eyes and let out a groan. "Shouldn't have done that."

"Are you okay?"

"Confused and trying to beat this headache."

"Because?"

"It hurts."

She sighed. "I meant the confusion."

"It's the house thing." When he spoke again, his voice dipped even lower. He rubbed his temples as he talked. "It's not possible."

"It's a fact."

"That doesn't make sense." He grabbed his head as he spoke.

"You really do have a headache, don't you?"

"There isn't anything that doesn't hurt, but I'd really like an explanation for the rental."

Her gaze swept over him. His bloody T-shirt lay wadded up in a ball on the floor. That left him bare-chested and, despite the injury and pale face, as formidable and dangerous as when he'd stepped behind her attacker hours ago.

"I'd show you the lease, but it's probably scorched, along with everything else I own."

He waved her off. "Not a big deal. Insurance will cover most of it."

"I hate when guys do that dismissive thing."

His hands fell to the mattress. "How did I do that?"

"What about my memories? Nothing expensive or even important to anyone but me, but they're still mine." The photographs of her family and the diaries she'd kept since she turned twelve. She knew being alive was a miracle, but she mourned the moments she would now only carry in her head.

"But it's only stuff."

"Never mind." A practical guy who carried light would never understand, so she didn't even try. "Why do you doubt my renting status?"

"Because I own the house with Garrett. Because we never agreed to rent. Because he never mentioned you. Because I can't believe Sara would agree."

"I see you've given this some thought."

"I've been stuck on an assignment in Arizona, but I'd think Garrett would have gotten word to me."

"This assignment of yours." Her gaze wandered to the nightstand and the two guns, one knife and strange-looking metal star thing sitting there. "I guess it explains the weapons?"

"Remember how I said I was a Border Patrol agent? Well, I've been undercover for fourteen months."

"Sounds terrible."

His mouth fell into a flat line when he tried to sit up higher on the bed. He flopped back against the pillow as the skin around the corners of his mouth turned white. "It was even worse than that, but it's over."

"No wonder you seem so comfortable chasing and shooting."

"Not so good with being injured, though."

She traced her fingers over the edge of the bandage and watched his stomach dip in response. "You got knifed on your last assignment. It hadn't healed when the guy hit you."

"And now I am on mandatory leave."

The laugh bubbled up before she could stop it. "This is your idea of rest and relaxation? Dodging bullets and running from fires?"

"Believe it or not, no."

His broad smile caught her off guard. Since she'd done enough admiring of his strong jaw and sexy mouth, she looked around the room, anywhere not to stare at him.

The room smelled like wet carpet, and the dark brown furniture and lack of sunlight made it resemble a tomb. Not the best place for a guy to recuperate.

They both jumped when Joel opened the door, talking as he walked. "Pax and Davis are on the way."

She drew back her hand and inched away from Jeremy. "Who?"

"More of Garrett's men." This time Jeremy scooted back until his neck rested against the headboard. "Why are they even here? I thought they were working out east these days."

"Had some business in town."

Jeremy nodded. "Understood."

"That makes one of us." The shortcut conversation was making her crazy. She'd shoot them her best eye roll but was too tired to do anything but talk, and even that took more concentration than she possessed. "Now might be a good time to tell me what your brother does and why he has so many men helping him do it."

"I like her." Joel laughed as he took up a position by the window, glancing at them each in turn and then looking outside. "Don't get me wrong. I liked Sara, too, but this one has spunk."

That was the second or third time Meredith had heard the name. Each time Jeremy had frowned and shot her an unreadable look.

Meredith couldn't shake the feeling of being judged by Jeremy. "And while you're at it, explain who this Sara person is."

Joel treated her to the typical she-lost-it look guys did so well. "She's Garrett's fiancée."

Meredith jumped off the bed. Nearly swallowed her tongue and bounced Jeremy off the mattress as she moved. "His what?"

"I guess I should say ex. I mean, you guys are—" Joel's smirk died. "Right?"

"Wrong."

Jeremy wrapped his fingers around her wrist and gave her a gentle tug until she looked down at him. "You still sure you're not seeing Garrett?"

"Positive. Never dated or even thought about it."

Jeremy pointed at his mouth. "You can resist a face like this?"

"On Garrett, yes. Keep in mind he was never around."

Jeremy's hold tightened before he let his hand drop. "Go back to your first comment. Only on my brother?"

She'd hoped he'd missed that verbal misstep. No such luck. "I'm wondering why I've never seen this Sara person at the house."

The amusement faded from Jeremy's eyes. "I'm worried about the same thing."

Joel held up his phone. "She didn't answer any of the four times I've tried."

Meredith refused to panic. None of the information she'd heard made any sense. She rarely saw Garrett, but he'd never mentioned a fiancée and never bothered to bring her by to say hello. The pieces refused to fit together in any logical way. Still, Meredith had to believe a reasonable explanation lingered somewhere, maybe just out of reach, but there. "Couldn't she be on vacation with Garrett? That would explain why we can't reach either of them."

Something cold and bleak moved behind Jeremy's

eyes. He controlled the starkness almost immediately. "I can't contact him through any of our regular channels and he's not answering the emergency call signal."

Joel shook his head. "Damn."

From the reaction, she knew the lack of communication wasn't standard. She might not see him for weeks, but Garrett clearly checked in with Jeremy and the team. The failure to do so now had the other men reeling. Their tension touched off a new round of swirling panic inside her.

"Tell Pax and Davis to search for Sara. Credit cards, bank records. I want to know where she's been." Jeremy reached for his phone and frowned when it wasn't in its place on the nightstand. "Once I fight off this painkiller buzz, I'll check her house and some other places where she might be."

Meredith put her hand over her back pocket. If Jeremy saw the bulge he'd know she'd grabbed his cell. He'd likely jump to conclusions about her wanting to call for help. In reality she knew, deep down knew, she was safest with Jeremy and there was no reason to run.

She also knew she had to hide his phone if she wanted him to rest. Having all those muscles meant nothing if he passed out at her feet.

"Already ahead of you on the calls," Joel said. "Davis and I will take surveillance. Pax is coming to check you out."

"Not necessary." Jeremy shifted to the side of the bed.

She moved to lean against the mattress, blocking his path to the floor. "Does this Pax have medical training?"

Joel smiled. "Yes, ma'am."

"Then I like your plan. Pax stays. You remain in bed for now." She nudged Jeremy until he fell back onto the bed.

"Since when are you in charge?" Jeremy asked as he closed his eyes and leaned into the pillows.

No way was she conceding even an inch in this verbal battle. "Since you lost a pint or two of blood."

Joel cleared his throat as he opened the door. "I'll wait outside while you two hash this out."

She didn't wait to ask the question burning a hole in her brain. "Why would Garrett hide a fiancée?"

Jeremy didn't open his eyes. "No idea."

"Did you think they were still together?"

"They were having trouble but…" His eyes popped open. "I'll feel better when I find her and Garrett."

"Let's get back to his job. Who exactly is your brother?" Then they could circle around to Jeremy's job, as well, before the curiosity ate a hole in Meredith's stomach.

She wasn't ready to let the issue drop with a cursory explanation. Something these men did had gotten them in trouble, and as a result she was homeless with nothing more than the clothes she wore. She didn't blame them. Not specifically. But she wasn't going to be pushed aside either.

"Are you rapid firing questions to keep me from having a second to change your orders to Joel about fetching Pax?" he asked.

*Smart man.* "That and to get an answer or two out of you while your defenses are down."

"Effective."

She crossed her arms over her stomach. "It will be once you answer me."

He stared at her. When she didn't move or even break eye contact, he exhaled long and loud. "Garrett's job is top secret."

Not exactly the comment she was expecting. "How very Hollywood of you to say that."

"It's true."

She dropped her hands to her sides. "Jeremy, come on. After everything that's happened today, the least you can do is level with me. I think I deserve better than the 'if I tell you I'll have to kill you' nonsense."

"It's not my secret to tell."

"What, you think this has all been an elaborate scheme to get you to give up information on your brother's job?"

The silence stretched out long enough to be comical. Finally, he gave a clipped response. "No."

"You have trust issues."

"DIA."

It took her a second to realize he'd given her the answer. Well, an answer. Not that she understood what he said. "I don't even know what that is."

"Defense Intelligence Agency."

"Never heard of it. The name I know starts with a *C.* "

"He collects military-related foreign intel."

The extra information didn't bring any clarity. "Is he in the military?"

"Former army sergeant."

"And now?"

"Black ops stuff."

The curt responses raised more questions than they answered. Instead of calming the racing in her stomach, his comments kicked the churning to top speed. "That explains the travel."

"It also means it's not that easy to find him when he wants to stay missing."

"I was afraid you were going to say that."

# Chapter Six

Bruce Casden stared across the table at his five-hundred-dollar-per-hour lawyer, Stephen Simmons. The Third. Simmons never forgot to add that annoying reminder of his old-money family whenever he introduced himself.

Even now, framed by the dingy gray of cement prison block walls, Simmons acted as if he sat in the middle of a country club, all stiff with his perfect posture. The designer glasses and tailored suit—Bruce had paid for it all. The guy threw in the condescending smile free of charge.

Simmons never understood how the people Bruce knew could alter the look of a man's face. Use a razor to change the curve of his chin or take off an ear. A knife to blind him.

Bruce knew people. The kind of people who never dreamed about someday going to college because the idea was so outside the mean streets they lived on. Bruce knew that neighborhood. Had escaped it but never forgotten how it lurked in another part of town, just waiting to drag him back in.

The idea of seeing certain body parts of Simmons rearranged and that smug mouth twisted in pain made Bruce smile. His current situation, sitting in a windowless room with the prospect of a soulless cell as his new living quarters, sucked the amusement right back out of him.

He stared at the thick steel door that locked them in together, glanced at the gold ring on Simmons's pinkie as it caught the fluorescent lights. Armed guards lingered in the sterile hallway just outside the door. Their presence likely filled Simmons with a sense of security. Little did he know Bruce could snap his neck before the uniformed simpletons fumbled over each other and slipped the security card in the reader to open the door.

"Why am I still in here and not at my office desk?" Bruce asked.

"The government is taking a special interest in your case."

"That's not news. This is the third time one of my businesses has been raided."

Simmons's mouth turned up in a fake smile filled with loathing. "And the first time they found something, which is the problem."

"I'm a businessman with commercial properties in Arizona and California." Bruce repeated the spiel he'd been practicing for so long. "I'm not in each office and warehouse every day and certainly can't be expected to know what the employees there are doing. As you know, it's very hard to find motivated and honest employees these days."

Simmons hesitated before flipping through the pages tacked to his file. When he stopped on one, his finger slid across the page as his eyes scanned the lines of black print. "The agents claim they found seventeen tons of marijuana in the storage room of your warehouse."

"And I will question everyone who works for me until I uncover the identity of the person who—"

"They also found a drug-smuggling tunnel leading from the furnace room of your strip mall into Mexico."

Bruce's back teeth slammed together. "Don't interrupt me."

Simmons's head shot up. "What?"

"I'm paying you enough to never interrupt me when I speak. Do not do it again."

The chair creaked when Simmons leaned back. His stomach pulled at the buttons of his shirt and hung over his belt. "You don't seem to understand how serious these charges are."

Bruce knew. He also knew they would never stick without the necessary witness. The evidence bags could go missing. Forensics could be corrupted. Eliminating a witness took more subtlety.

While prison might provide the perfect alibi, Bruce missed his bed. "Get me out of here."

"It's not that easy."

"I pay you to make things run smoothly. Right now, you're not earning your fee."

"The bail hearing is tomorrow."

"I do not intend to spend even one night in an Arizona jail. In any jail, for that matter."

Simmons continued as if Bruce hadn't spoken. "If we are successful there will be some restrictions on your travel."

"I have business at one of my properties in San Diego."

"One of your managers will need to handle it for you. There is no way you can cross state lines."

"This is the sort of job a smart man doesn't trust to others. According to a recent call, the last time I tried everything fell apart." Bruce rubbed his hands together, imagining how good it would feel to use his hands for something away from his desk and the signing of agreements. He ached for action. His blood raced and heated at the idea of settling this debt on his own.

Simmons tapped his shiny pen against the scarred table. "People are tired of the drug trade and drug-related violence."

*The whining masses.* "I'm not interested in public morality. I develop strip malls. My only sin is in helping people to shop. I had no idea anything nefarious was occurring."

Between the dramatic exhale and the way he slapped the file shut, Simmons telegraphed his disgust. "We need to work on your story."

"The Border Patrol agent set me up."

"His record is rock solid."

The tightness in Bruce's stomach eased. The idea of destroying the agent who had broken protocol and infiltrated his operation unknotted the ball of tension that had been growing and spinning since the agents had landed on his doorstep with weapons drawn. "Which will make his downfall all the more compelling and the charges easier to throw out."

"He's an integral part of the case, but—"

"Then we'll be fine."

The briefcase slapped against the table and the locks clicked open as Simmons rifled around inside. "You're very sure of your position. I'm not sure if that's good or bad."

"I understand people."

Narrowed brown eyes peeked over the leather lid of the case. "What does that mean?"

"Simple."

Simmons closed the briefcase and leaned his elbows on the top. "Explain it to me."

"Mr. Hill won't be a problem much longer."

JEREMY GRABBED THE cotton shirt off the top of the bag Joel had dumped on the floor before he headed out with Davis.

At least the three guys had stopped standing around staring at him. Jeremy had almost blown his cool over the petri dish treatment.

Except for Meredith. She could stare all she wanted. Look, touch, smile and crawl right up on his lap. She'd likely kick a little butt as she did it, but he didn't mind any of the options if they came at her hands.

It would be a long time before he forgot the bone-deep determination in her eyes and snapping through every part of her as she'd pushed with all her might against his side to stop the bleeding. Even through the red haze of pain, he'd felt her willing him to survive.

Before he knew it, a man could forfeit his common sense for a woman like her.

He slipped the shirt over his shoulders and winced when the move sent a sharp tug down to his side. "Hate getting stabbed."

"Normal people do." Meredith sat on the bed next to him, rubbing her hands together and fidgeting. She didn't reach over and button his shirt, but it sure looked as if she wanted to.

To keep from doing something stupid like putting his hands on her as *he* wanted to, he looked at Pax. Yeah, that killed all thoughts of dragging Meredith down on the mattress and thanking her.

Then Jeremy saw the needle. "Put that away."

"You need to rest. My job is to make sure you do it. Do you know how tempting it is to knock you out?" Pax, six feet tall with shoulders wider than the doorway, tapped his finger against the syringe.

The guy could crush a car in his hands and ignored most orders, but he was behaving now. Acting as if he moved in society all the time, which he didn't.

Jeremy guessed Meredith's presence caused the change

from Pax's usual paranoid style. He'd been an army medic. Now he worked on a contract basis for Garrett, who had once said he'd brought the Weeks brothers in when the job seemed impossible, when the team was balanced on the verge of elimination with only hope and spit holding them together.

Like Garrett, Pax and Davis excelled at the impossible. They not only survived, they thrived as the pressure increased to crushing levels.

Pax moved, his smile growing with each step. "I can either sedate you or get my wish and use my fist to knock you on your—"

"Neither. I have to find my brother."

"We'll take care of that while you sleep it off."

Jeremy did a quick assessment. He mentally calculated the distance to the door and how fast he could get there with only one side of his body at normal strength. Didn't take a genius to figure out there was no way to win his way out of this using brute force. Not when a guy built like a wall stood in front of him, and Meredith balanced on the edge of the bed as if ready to pounce if needed.

No, Jeremy had to use his smarts if he hoped to win this one. "If Davis were lost, would you leave the rescue to someone else?"

"I would if I couldn't walk without falling down."

Meredith nodded as Pax spoke.

Jeremy ignored them both. Sometimes playing it safe and following the rules didn't work. This was one of those times. "I have to find him."

"I'll head over to Sara's house, then check in with Davis and Joel. In the meantime, you'll rest." Pax waved the needle in the air in an unspoken threat.

Jeremy held up his hands in what he hoped looked like surrender. "You win."

Pax put a hand behind his ear and leaned in, exaggerating the moment and making Meredith smile. "What was that?"

"You don't need that. I get it. No moving."

Meredith stood up, adding her five-foot-six to the already imposing human blockade. "I'll make sure he doesn't move."

Pax looked her over from head to foot before a smile pulled at the corner of his mouth. "I actually think you're tough enough to do it."

"Comes with the territory."

He frowned. "Are you Border Patrol, too?"

"Meaner than that. I'm an elementary school teacher."

"Ah." Pax hesitated before easing his finger off the syringe's stopper. He clipped a plastic cover over the needle and put the sedative back in his bag. "Rough gig."

That was enough talking as far as Jeremy was concerned. For his plan to work, Pax needed to leave. "She lived with Garrett before her house turned to kindling."

The scowls came at him from Pax and Meredith. Pulsing tension replaced the previous calm in the room.

"But not like that." Her frown could melt metal. "Stop trying to switch the attention from you to me."

Pax waved his hand in front of his face. "Hey, that's none of my business anyway. I don't judge."

"Maybe not, but I want the record clear." The scowl stayed on her mouth and her gaze never left Jeremy. "Neighbors only. Nothing romantic ever happened with Garrett."

Pax laughed. "That's a shame for Garrett."

*Yeah, more than enough talking or whatever this was.* Jeremy lay back on the pillows Meredith had stacked behind him. "You can go, Pax."

"Right." The amusement hadn't left the other man's voice.

Jeremy didn't find the situation all that funny, but he did appreciate the help. "Thanks, man."

Meredith followed Pax to the door. He turned and handed her a piece of paper. "You might need this."

She slipped Jeremy's phone out of her back pocket and started punching in the numbers.

"How did you get that? I wondered where my phone went," he mumbled, now knowing to watch her hands while he watched the rest of her.

She peeked up at him. "I'm not stupid. I stole it."

"No, you aren't." Just one more thing about her that fascinated him.

She closed the door and leaned back against it, staring him down. "I don't buy for one second that you've given up your plans to run out of here."

"I see we understand each other." He sat up and whistled as a rough breath hissed through his teeth. "I'd leave you here, but I'm not convinced it's safe, despite the out-of-the-way location. So be ready to go in ten minutes."

"You better mean that you need help getting to the bathroom."

For a second he wondered if the attraction sparked in only one direction. Nothing sexy about bathroom talk unless she meant a shower, and he knew she didn't. "Definitely not."

"Get back into bed." She pointed as she walked. The stern look, the clear voice, it all said teacher.

School hadn't been his favorite thing, except for gym class and the football team, but a teacher who looked like her might have made him reassess his limited time in the library. "There's somewhere we need to look for Sara."

"Let the other guys do it."

"They don't know about this place."

Meredith sat down next to him and braced a hand on the opposite side of his legs. "You could tell them."

Any other time he'd love being straddled by her, but right now he had to find Sara. "Logical, but not an option."

"Care to tell me why?"

"Can't."

"More top secret ridiculous spy stuff?"

"The word you're looking for is *operative.*"

"It all sounds like a line to me."

Meredith was not going to let it go and he couldn't blame her. He'd never have bought this spy crap if she'd tried to sell it to him. "It's a safe house. A place Sara knew to go if everything else fell apart."

Meredith sat back up, taking her weight off him. "But why would she go there if she was no longer seeing Garrett?"

The woman asked good questions. Logical questions. But common sense had no place in gut reactions. "I don't have an answer. All I have is a hunch."

"How do you plan to get there? We don't have a car."

He'd forgotten about the transportation issue. He couldn't exactly call a cab, and asking any of the guys for keys would tip them off. But he did have a backup. He always had a backup.

She didn't say "I told you so," but her smile said it for her. "Guess that settles that."

As if he'd let a little thing like car theft stop him. Luckily he didn't have to resort to that. "We'll borrow one."

It was her turn to look stunned. Her eyes bulged. "You mean steal."

"We'll bring it right back. Well, eventually. Unless we accidentally wreck it."

Her eyes narrowed. "Are you kidding?"

"Actually, yes. There's a car stashed in the falling-down groundskeeper shed. It's old but it runs. We'll use that." The way her skin flushed and her eyes got all fiery when she prepared for battle made him hotter than he cared to admit. It was spooky how much he enjoyed watching her. "Make sense?"

She started shaking her head before he finished the sentence. "No, nothing about this plan does."

"I can't let anything happen to Sara."

Meredith stilled. "You like her."

"Garrett *loves* her." Jeremy emphasized his brother's name. "That's all that matters to me. If he's not around to save her, I will."

"You should have started with that explanation. It's your best argument." Meredith stood up and raised an eyebrow in his direction. "Why are you still sitting?"

Relief plowed into him. He almost hated to ruin the feeling but he had no choice. "I need to give you a few obligatory warnings about staying back and listening to orders."

"Not until you give me a weapon."

He'd rather tie her to the bed and leave her there. For more reasons than one....

A novice with a gun was a dangerous combination. He didn't even worry for his safety, but she could shoot herself or be attacked for holding the weapon, and the possibility of that made him sick. He couldn't take the risk. "Absolutely not."

She didn't even flinch. "I go armed or we stay here."

He recognized the tone. Firm and sure and not budging an inch. Still, being a confident woman was not enough. Her attitude didn't stand a chance against a bullet. "Are you sure you can shoot?"

"Yes."

Not the response he expected. "A person?"

"Yes."

"How do you know?"

"I know."

Against every ounce of common sense inside him, he handed her a weapon. "It's a semiautomatic. You shoot and it reloads. You'll have eight bullets, and be prepared for flying cartridges."

"I've used a semiautomatic before and know how the magazines work."

He had to ask. Not knowing was killing him. "You've practiced, what, once or twice?"

"I've shot about four thousand rounds, the most recent time being about five days ago." She held out her hand palm up. "The gun, please."

A whole new side of her opened up to him. He wanted to know more. "Is there anything you want to tell me about your past or your life outside the classroom?"

She inched her hand closer to him. "If we want to find Sara before midnight, you need to find me a gun and we need to go."

## Chapter Seven

A half hour later Meredith stood in front of a firehouse garage somewhere in downtown San Diego not far from PETCO Park, the baseball stadium. A rusty lock secured the metal brace to the brick wall of the building. A chain-link fence surrounded the property but its bent bottom didn't exactly shout safety. The black graffiti scrawled across the twenty-foot-high double doors didn't inspire confidence either.

"This is it?" She froze when the broken bulb of the safety light crunched under her foot.

Jeremy leaned one shoulder against the wall. "The point of a safe house is to blend."

She glanced down the abandoned street and rows of falling-down garages. "Define 'blend.'"

He chuckled. "The neighborhood is in transition."

"The place looks abandoned."

"Then we set it up right. It's the perfect cover."

"If you say so."

When he threw an arm around her shoulder and pressed her tight against his side, her heart sped up to a hyper rat-a-tat beat. With his hair damp from his quick wash-up after the medical attention, he brushed his cheek against hers.

"There are two cameras at the top of the building and

across the street." The volume of his voice dipped low. "We monitor the entire place all the time."

"Is someone here?"

His gaze bounced all around them as every inch of him went still. "Why, do you see something?"

"I'm wondering why you're whispering?"

"Just in case."

When she tried to look up, he gave her a small squeeze she assumed meant not to move. "That seems to be your justification for a lot of things."

He pointed at the chained door. "The rust is fake and the fence could stop a truck. There are motion sensors and all the images go to monitors at Garrett's office and directly to our phones."

"Very stealthy." And a bit scary.

The over-the-top security both stopped the nerves jumping around in her throat and set her back teeth chattering. Being here went against every minute of training she'd invested in. She never left public places when meeting with a man she didn't know. For Jeremy, she made an exception. The question was, why? And she really couldn't come up with a reasonable answer.

Even injured, with a slight limp from protecting his wounded side, he struck her as being twice as tough as any guy she'd ever met, including Garrett. The dark scowl gave him a sexy in-control look, but his smile… Oh, yeah. The way the corner of his mouth kicked up lit up his whole face, even as it sucked the air right out of her lungs.

Over the past few hours she'd glanced over only to find him staring back at her. He didn't turn away or pretend he hadn't seen her gaze. He met her eyes with a heated look of his own.

Garrett had walked in and out of her life and filled the role of helpful neighbor during those times when he wasn't absent. Even though the siblings shared identical looks, Jeremy's impact on her senses surpassed routine and sped straight toward explosive. There was nothing sisterly about the little dance in her stomach every time she looked at his face.

"I knew Garrett had many secrets, but a twin brother and all this covert equipment is a surprise."

"I'll take that as a compliment." Jeremy took the key-card out of his pocket.

"Where did you get that?"

"I always carry it. Slipped it out of my wallet back at the motel. Here, take this back. I should have just let you keep it at the motel." He turned her hand over and laid his cell in her palm. "And now for the impressive part."

She'd spent almost every minute with him being impressed. It took only a short time for her to figure out the truth. He stayed calm. He remained focused. He hunted the bad guys and wanted to save Sara because that's who he was. He never questioned what should be done. He just did it.

He slipped his fingers underneath a brick and pulled out the row of grout. "Embedded reader."

"Caterpillar. See? I can say random words, too."

"You're hysterical." Before she could blink, he slid the card through the crack.

"What are you doing?"

"Getting access."

"To what?"

"The entry log."

He could have said anything, even used his shoe to call for a flying car and had it land in front of him, and she wouldn't have been more surprised. Instead, he hit a button on the phone and lines of black print filled the small screen.

She squinted, hoping the gibberish would make sense if the words blurred together then broke apart again. "I have no idea what that says."

"It's code. The important piece of information is that someone has been here. Is still here."

"Sara?"

"I hope. Or Garrett. Someone with access swiped a card, which is a good sign."

"How exactly?"

"No one tried to break in. The log shows one entry."

"Unless two people went in together."

He froze. "What?"

"Just stating the obvious."

For the shortest of blips, his guard wavered. From the slight slump of his shoulders to the hitch in his voice, she knew his mind wandered to that awful place of uncertainty where he didn't know if his brother lived or not.

She'd survived a similar darkness. In her bleakest moments, when the man she'd thought she loved switched from insults to threats, she'd feared not the end but the moment before the end, when she'd know which one of her breaths would be her last. Then she'd made a decision not to face the unknown horror for one more day. She'd bought a gun, learned to shoot, moved out...and rolled through the waves of panic that came every time the phone rang or footsteps sounded in the hallway.

She'd been nineteen and naive and so sure she'd found what people searched a lifetime to find. She never saw how disconnected from reality she'd become. But this, right here, with Jeremy, tasted and felt real. Terrifying and completely incomprehensible in her black-and-white mind, but real. She'd long ago lost her ability to read men and no longer trusted her judgment, but Jeremy made her want to believe.

With his arm bent and tucked against his side, he threaded the fingers of his other hand through hers. "You okay?"

Shaking her head, she snapped out of the past and fell back to the present. Those deep blue eyes held her until her stomach bounced.

"Fine." She turned her attention to the boarded-up front door. Anything not to get lost in his gaze. "Do you own this building, too?"

"Garrett uses it for business." Jeremy felt behind the hinges. "Motion sensors." Another swipe of the card and the door opened, opposite to the way it would normally swing.

"If you're trying to impress me…"

His eyebrow rose. "Is it working?"

"Totally. Yes."

She followed, slipping in behind him as he entered the building. The door opened into a small metal-walled room. It looked like an entryway but there was no obvious way out except the door they'd just used. "I don't get it."

"Nothing is ever what it seems in Garrett's world. Or in mine, for that matter."

A lesson she knew all too well after her house had blown up. "You probably shouldn't say that to a woman you barely know. Doesn't exactly build trust."

Jeremy motioned to the wall in front of her. With a scrape, it started to rise. Darkness filled the edges of the dark cavern on the other side. Water dripped in the distance, mixing with the screech of the wall against its tracks. When it hit the halfway point, the backlit image in the middle of the room came into focus.

"Sara." Jeremy whispered the name as his hand dropped from around her and his gun appeared in a flash.

"Do not move, Mr. Hill." The menacing voice ripped through the empty room and slapped her in the face.

A man dressed all in black stood with his arm wrapped around the neck of a petite blonde. More menacing was the gun aimed at her head. Fear radiated off her as her chest rose and fell on hard thumping breaths. Her fingers clawed at her attacker's forearm and tears flooded her eyes.

Meredith could feel the other woman's every breath and every drip of panic. This had to be Sara, which meant they'd arrived too late.

"Garrett." Tension held the woman's jaw tight as she spoke.

Meredith could tell the difference between the brothers. It was more than an issue of hairstyle. The distinctions ranged from the cadence of their steps to the subtle shades in their facial expressions. If Meredith knew, Sara knew. You couldn't love a man and not know. She was using Garrett's name for a reason, whatever it was.

"What do you want?" Jeremy took a step away from Meredith, but his gun didn't leave his side.

"Put your weapons on the floor. All of them." The man pointed his gun at Meredith. "And just who are you?"

When she tried to move forward, Jeremy put out his arm and signaled for her to stay still. "She stays with me. She's not involved in this."

"Then you shouldn't have brought her with you. Your mistake." The man braced his legs apart and shifted the gun until it aimed at Meredith's heart. "What's your name, and no games. Tell me what I want to know or Sara Paulson dies."

The shock of hearing Sara's full name for the first time broke Meredith out of her stunned silence. Fear rumbled through every part of her body. Her legs shook hard enough to knock her over. It took all her concentration to hold still. "Meredith."

"Hill, if you care about Meredith or Sara here, you'll dump those weapons now. I won't tell you again. Not when I have all these bullets with your name on them."

"Screw you."

"Since you know how to follow orders, I have to assume you don't think I'm serious." The attacker took an exaggerated sniff of Sara's hair. "Should I hurt one of these lovely ladies as proof? Maybe you're the type who prefers that sort of thing."

Jeremy stood there for another few seconds before his hand moved to the band on his arm. Bending his knees, he dropped two guns on the floor. "Now we can talk."

"Slide them over here."

"No."

"Maybe you need to learn the hard way." The man smiled as he tightened his arm and tipped Sara's head back. His mouth hovered right over her ear and their cheeks touched.

"Stop." One gun, then the other skidded across the cement toward the attacker but out of grabbing range.

"Nice try, but I'll take the one at your ankle and everything else you have on you."

"Garrett." The plea for help was clear from the wobble in Sara's voice.

Her hands shook and her eyes mirrored the fear clogging Meredith's throat, threatening to choke her. She had no idea how Sara kept on her feet.

"Satisfied?" Jeremy asked as he dumped a small gun and two knives to the floor.

"Now the shirt. Untuck. Let me see your skin."

"I'm not into that."

"You would be just the type to tape a weapon to your bare chest. I'm not taking any chances."

Jeremy braced his legs apart. He unbuttoned his shirt and let it hang loose at his sides. On anyone else the obedience and bare chest might signal weakness. Not Jeremy. His chest puffed, growing more formidable and impressive the longer he stood.

"Who are you?" he asked.

"Someone with a message for you. But first you have to do something for me." The man motioned for Jeremy to raise his hands. "Good. Now pick."

Jeremy frowned. "What?"

But Meredith understood. She'd been on the wrong end of a man determined to take down a woman before. Had seen the swirling sickness grow and pulse as he invented new ways to show his power.

All the helplessness came rushing back to her until dizziness shook her brain. The man planned to kill one of them. Either her or Sara.

"We have two women. You're one man, but you can't be greedy." The attacker pointed his gun at Meredith then at Sara. "Choose."

The muscles in Jeremy's face clenched. "You want me. Take me and let the women go."

"Thanks but I'll keep my leverage." The man pulled Sara in tighter against his side.

Jeremy's jaw tightened to the point of snapping. "Won't mean much when I kill you."

No empty boast here. Meredith heard the vow in the soft darkness of his voice. It should have shaken her, knocked her back and sent her into an emotional spasm that stopped her brain. Should have, but it didn't.

Security wrapped around her, filling her with a well-spring of strength. The kind that made her believe she could survive anything.

The attacker shook his head. "With what? I've left you defenseless."

"I'll only need my hands. Probably only one."

For the first time, the attacker's smug assurance fell. The smile disappeared. "Maybe I'll kill both women, then take you out."

The gun tucked into Meredith's belt rubbed against her back. The heat burned into her skin and the weight almost doubled her over.

She itched to stop this madness but had to get Sara out of striking range first. "Let Sara go and take me."

Sara whimpered.

Jeremy sent a heart-stopping look of pure fury over his shoulder. "Do not move from that spot."

Doubt crashed through Meredith's adrenaline rush. "I have to."

The attacker wiped his mouth over Sara's cheek. "What a brave lady you are, Meredith. I'm sure Sara would agree if she could talk without crying."

"I think I'll have a better chance of survival than she will," Meredith said, not wanting to give any part of her plan away.

The attacker barked out a harsh laugh. "Against a bullet?"

"I'm bigger, so likely stronger." Except for her knees, which turned to mush and refused to move.

"You'll bleed the same. Everyone does." The attacker stared at Jeremy. Whatever he saw there had him nodding in agreement. "Fine. I accept your terms, pretty Meredith. You get to die, though it would have been entertaining to see Garrett sweat and squirm as he weighed the value of one woman over the other."

The attacker loosened his vise grip around Sara's neck. Red marks marred her skin and her body shook as she struggled out of his grasp. He wasn't ready to let go. He held her elbow, shifting her body in front of his like a shield.

The weasel.

Meredith inhaled, forcing every last drop of energy in her body to her feet to get them to move. One sliding step, then another.

"No!" Jeremy blocked her body with his.

Always protecting. Always sacrificing.

She put her hand on his forearm and shifted until she stood beside him. If she could get in front of him, he'd see the gun. She'd duck and he could shoot over her head. Playing musical positions would give them a chance to save Sara and possibly get out of there alive.

Rather than read her mind, Jeremy went with plan B. As soon as Sara moved, so did he. A dark blur passed in front of her as he dived for the attacker. Sara jumped to the side as the attacker let go and changed targets. With a mouth twisted in a feral snarl, he aimed his weapon at Jeremy in midlunge.

Before her brain could signal a message to her fingers, Meredith reached behind her back and whipped out the gun. Remembering all of her shooting lessons, keeping her focus on the one man she wanted dead and off the other she hoped to save, she squeezed the trigger, eyes open and hands steady. The booms thundered over the men's shouts.

*Bang. Bang.*

The cartridges pinged against the hard floor. The kick vibrated through her arm, but she ignored the unexpected twinge of muscle pain.

The attacker switched his gaze to her a bit too late. The

red-faced haze morphed into openmouthed surprise. Then he dropped to the floor with his eyes open and a blossom of red spreading over his chest.

Jeremy slammed to a halt. He grabbed empty air as the man hit the ground at his feet. His body deflated as his speed went from sixty to zero.

Jeremy spun around and stared at her. "What the…?"

She couldn't move. Desperation pounded through her. Her arms were frozen in front of her and she couldn't drop the gun despite trying to shake her hold loose.

The trembling started in her feet and worked up to her shoulders and every cell inside her screamed with the need to collapse to the floor. If only her mind would click back on.

With a shaking voice, he took a step toward her. "Meredith?"

A high-pitched scream split the silence before she could answer. The pain filling the keening cry made Meredith want to fold her hands over her ears and curl in a ball in a corner.

Sara beat her to it. She stood over the dead body. All color drained from her face and her mouth hung open as the terror poured out of her.

Jeremy looked from Meredith to Sara and back again.

More than anything, Meredith needed him to rush to her side, to take her in his arms. He could peel her fingers off the gun and tell her it would somehow all be okay. A soft caress, a brush of lips against her temple. She wanted it all. The shocking need didn't make sense, but she craved his touch and attention.

He reached for Sara.

# Chapter Eight

Jeremy battled an uncharacteristic case of uncertainty. He was the guy who went in first. He didn't question. He didn't hesitate to put his life on the line if he had to. He'd taken an oath he viewed as sacred. But nothing had prepared him for the stark despair bordering on pleading in the women's eyes.

His heart ached for Meredith as she stood statue-still with the gun aimed at the now empty space in the middle of the room. She'd made the right decision, regardless of the danger. Her instincts proved to be as good as any of the agents he fought beside on the drug battlefields in Arizona.

But the why of her actions wouldn't matter as she crawled into bed each night. This memory would linger. She'd forever be one of those who knew what it cost to pull the trigger.

He wanted to go to her, to thank her for saving his life and being stronger than he ever gave her credit for, but Sara needed him more. She wasn't weak, but violence had never tainted her world. Meredith clearly had not experienced the same dose of luck.

Sara's knees buckled. He saw her crumple and grabbed her before she hit the floor. His body absorbed her chill as he balanced her hip against his.

"Sara? Talk to me."

"I'm okay." The shock bleached her skin white as she fought through shallow breaths. Fingernails dug into his arm. "Where's Garrett?"

For those few minutes Jeremy's attention had focused solely on the women. He hadn't let his mind slip off to that indescribable place where none of his questions had answers and his fears about Garrett's absence didn't attack his brain.

Now the slicing terror returned. It clogged his throat until he had to force the words out around it. "Wasn't he with you?"

"No." She shook her head as she steadied her shoulders and stood on her own again. "I got the signal and—"

"Signal?"

It was the first word he'd heard from Meredith since she'd fired the gun. Her hand now hung loose at her side. The determination on her flat lips hadn't diminished one bit.

He closed the gap between the two women, bringing Sara along with him until he stood within touching distance of both of them. "Meredith Samms, this is Sara Paulson."

"Does she know?" Force moved back into Sara's voice. Gone was the wilting flower. Her shoulders snapped back. Her eyes were alert as she watched Meredith.

Jeremy wasn't exactly sure what was happening, but expected this sizing up was inevitable after all the confidentiality lectures Sara had been forced to endure from Garrett. But that didn't mean Jeremy couldn't defuse the situation.

"About Garrett's job? Yeah, as much as she can. I filled her in."

"Why?" Sara asked.

"I'm starting to wonder that myself," Meredith mumbled.

Jeremy leaned closer to Meredith. The move didn't satisfy his thumping need to know what put that wariness in her eyes, but it did send the silent signal he wanted. She was with him and Sara should not question that fact. "Speaking of my brother?"

Sara shot Meredith one last questioning frown before turning to Jeremy. "It's been more than a month since I talked with Garrett, but when I got the emergency text I came here as we practiced. I thought maybe he wanted to…"

"What?"

She waved Jeremy off. "It doesn't matter. Point is I didn't see or hear anyone, but when I went to swipe the card to get in this guy came at me." She stared as if lost in the memory.

He glanced at Meredith for direction but she was too busy looking at Sara with sad eyes now filled with concern.

"Sara?" He dipped his head to try to get eye contact.

She rubbed her forehead and the haze hovering over her eyes cleared. "The guy jumped me. Told me to get him in the building or he'd kill Garrett. I was in there forever, just standing, with him not saying anything until you showed up."

"And you recognized me and not Garrett." Jeremy knew that was true. Sara could always tell, even in those days when they both wore government-regulation haircuts.

Meredith snorted. "Of course she did."

"I thought using the wrong name might buy some time and send you a message," Sara said at the same time.

"The gun aimed at your head did that." And if he never saw that again, he'd die a happy man.

"I really thought I'd see Garrett." Sara's face fell in a look that could only be described as bewildered. "That he'd been lured there and I'd have to sit there and watch him die."

Meredith put a hand on Sara's arm as she looked at Jeremy. "Where is Garrett?"

"Who are you again? I don't understand where you fit in." The question hung in both Sara's voice and the way she watched Meredith. There was no judgment, but no trust either.

"She's with me. She's a good friend of mine." Jeremy didn't break eye contact with Meredith as he staked his claim.

She didn't even flinch.

From the husky voice to the battle-warrior spirit, she held him in a trance. Her depth surprised him. She was more than an elementary school teacher. He respected the career choice but doubted weapons training was a part of the regular classroom curriculum. Darkness and light played inside her in a mystery he vowed to unravel.

Sara's head fell to the side, spilling her hair over her shoulder. "Do you work with Jeremy?"

"No." That was it. Meredith didn't say anything else or add any details that could have tipped Sara off or tripped them all up.

Since Meredith's connection to him was through Garrett, and since Jeremy suspected Sara didn't know about the living arrangements that had led to Meredith being dragged into this mess, Jeremy followed her lead. There was plenty of time for Sara to find out about Garrett's secret and very confusing life when he was away from her. While he was at it, he could explain it to his brother.

"Now isn't the best time for explanations. We need—" His phone vibrated. Not to indicate an incoming call. No, this was an alert. A warning he could not ignore.

That fast Meredith was over his shoulder and staring at the screen with him. "What now?"

He tapped in the password and an image of the outer entry came into view. The door to the outside stood open and two figures loomed in the small space on the other side of the hidden door. In a move that appeared practiced, neither faced the security cameras.

Jeremy couldn't see their weapons but he knew they had them. "Trouble."

Meredith blew out a long breath. "More men are coming."

"They're actually here." And he might need her shooting skills to survive the next few minutes, so he didn't pretty up the facts. "Present tense."

"For the record, I've had better first dates."

His racing mind screeched to a halt. So much for concentrating on the problem at hand.

He looked down at her. "Is that what this is?"

Sara tugged on his arm. "Wait, you just met her and she knows about Garrett?"

"We can figure out the definitions and work out all the explanations later." Meredith grabbed Jeremy's wrist and watched the image of the men moving around the closed-in room. "You need to pick up your weapons."

No one had ever had to tell him that before. The circumstances, dealing with Meredith, it all had him reeling.

"Right." He collected them, returning each to its hiding place. "We need to go."

He motioned for them to gather around him, spotting movement along the back wall more than thirty feet away. Gray seeped under the huge sliding door at the opposite end of the room. Smoke curled up toward the ceiling and danced along the walls just as the smell of burning walls hit him.

That blocked that exit.

"Fire?" Panic filled Meredith's voice.

Sara shook her head. "It can't be."

Meredith looked around the room, her movements jerky as her gaze went to the staircase in the corner across from the fire. "Is there another way out from up there?"

"That's the problem." The safe house that once seemed so logical now had Jeremy kicking his own butt. The large, wide-open room lacked crevices, places to duck and wait. "The loft is our only choice. We'll be able to see anyone going in or out from up there and get a few extra minutes of fresh air. It's an advantage we need."

Meredith stopped spinning around and looked at him. "I'm sensing a 'but' in there."

"The area has the essentials, but we'll be trapped. There's no exit and the smoke will rise. We go up the stairs and we'll need to get back down as soon as we can clear a path."

"Interesting layout choice."

"Yeah, we intended to fix it and install a crawl-out but neither of us have been around long enough to accomplish the task." Jeremy saw the attackers huddle together near the base of the door. If they were clever enough to breach the outside entrance, they'd be inside within minutes. "Upstairs *now.*"

He shuffled the women toward the stairs as the fire built to a roar outside the back doors. The temperature spiked all around them. Being inside the equivalent of a metal box kept the heat in. Soon, touching the walls would sear their skin off.

With a nod from Jeremy, Meredith led the charge up

the stairs, her sneakers clomping against the metal. When she got to the top, she held out a hand and pulled Sara up behind her.

He'd made it to the middle of the steps when the bottom of the unit's steel door started to rise. Smoke painted the room in a coughing haze, but he could see feet and knew their time was up. Sprinting up the last two stairs, he landed on the floor fifteen feet above the ground. Meredith and Sara huddled on the floor against the bed, out of sight from the area below.

As the door creaked and shimmied, the emergency lights blinked off. Jeremy let his eyes adjust, then conducted a final inventory of the small space around them. They had only the bed and small chair for protection.

Crawling on his stomach, he reached the edge of the mattress frame and looked at Meredith. "Give me a hand."

Without words, they flipped over the mattress and pressed it against the warming wall as a buffer from the stifling heat. The chair crashed on its side against the floor as they set up a mock fortress with the frame and box spring pressed against the overturned seat.

He pushed the women down and inside the bunker as his body shook from a smoke-induced coughing fit. "Do not move unless I tell you."

Meredith grabbed his hand with one of hers as she used the other to cover her mouth. "You can't do this alone."

Part of him knew she was right, but he would not put her in even bigger danger. If he went down she still had a chance. The attackers wouldn't be expecting her to come out shooting, and he now knew she would. "Put the pillows over your mouths to filter the air and stay low."

He grabbed the railing around the loft and lowered his body to the floor. He'd just checked his weapon when he felt Meredith's breath against his cheek and her weight on his back.

"Let me help."

"No." When she looked like she was about to argue, he pressed a finger against her lips. "I'm the first line on this."

"And if you die—" Meredith choked out the words over a stream of coughing "—Sara and I won't survive."

Shadows slipped under the door and into the smoke-filled darkness. The arguments no longer mattered. This was about battle. About the upper hand. "Start at the left side and shoot toward the middle. Spread bullets. I'll head in from the right."

They fell to their stomachs, both coughing from the vile air now, as gunfire boomed and pinged all around them. The men below shouted directions and shoes squeaked against the floor. Jeremy fired again and heard a groan right before an outline crashed to the cement. "One down."

He shot until he ran out of bullets and had to grab a second gun and start over. Something shifted off to his left. He glanced over, expecting to unload a new round of ammunition, when he saw the newest problem. Flames traveled up the wall and licked the ceiling. The attackers clearly intended to smoke them out or kill them in a fire. Jeremy had no intention of picking either choice.

Over the thundering rumble, Jeremy heard the slap of footsteps and watched as more figures rolled under the door. Reality slapped him. They'd handled the first wave and now reinforcements had taken their place.

His lungs clenched as if a giant fist strangled them. He was outnumbered and running out of ammo. Meredith kept shooting, all of her focus centered on the shadows moving below even as her shoulders convulsed in a series of coughs, but one attacker neared the stairs.

"Stay here," he said.

"What are you—" She swiveled around, but he was gone.

He crouched at the top of the stairs and forced out all the distractions and fears about watching another woman die at his feet and settled his mind to the job in front of him. This wasn't like last time.

Unlike in Arizona, he could step in. This time didn't have to end like last time. No one would get up the stairs unless they shot their way through him first.

He picked off one guy as he rounded the bottom rail. He hit another who tried to storm up through the middle. When he turned to help Meredith cover the ground with bullets, all that greeted him was an empty click. Through the stifling smoke he saw the dead eyes of a man right below Meredith and set to fire.

Jeremy captured her in a diving tackle and rolled her to the side. Bullets tore through the floor right where she'd been laying and the fiery booms kept coming. He crowded her against the scorching wall, trying to envelope her until his body received most of the impact.

Through the roar of blood in his ears, he heard a high-pitched beeping. It rose above the shouting, gunfire and raging flames. He couldn't place it or identify it. Not that it was important. He had to cover Meredith and grab for Sara.

A rumble built to a crushing bang. He looked up in time to see the door burst open. A blinding light flooded the room, cutting through the billowing smoke.

Meredith tried to raise her head, but Jeremy kept her tucked and locked under him, pushing her tighter to the floor. Through the blasts and yelling, he tried to focus. The shots rang out in one long string...then silence.

He lifted himself up on his elbows, coughing through the ash falling around them like a blanket. Keeping Meredith pinned to the floor, he crawled over and peered down to the floor below. He counted four bodies on the ground and two more on the stairs. Chunks of wall and discarded weapons littered the ground.

Two lights sat in the opening, highlighting two more men as they slipped inside. "Jeremy?"

That voice he knew. Garrett had come to the rescue.

The emergency lighting kicked on and water rained down from ceiling sprinklers and chemical fire retardant streamed from the hoses attached to the floor joists. Over Garrett's yelling, the puffs of smoke turned white as the flames hissed against the liquid assault.

Jeremy was never so grateful for Garrett's over-planning on security measures as he was right then.

After what felt like hours but probably only amounted to minutes in the thundering shower, Jeremy figured it was safe for them to move and for Garrett and his team to maneuver downstairs. Scrambling to his knees, Jeremy leaned over the rail and gazed into eyes identical to his own. Relief crashed into him from every angle. "We're up here."

Jeremy barely whispered the words, but his brother must have heard. His head tilted and he ran to the base of the stairs. "Are you okay?"

"Seems so."

"Where's Sara?"

"Here!" she screamed from the back of the loft. She got to the edge of the steps before Garrett grabbed her in a strangling bear hug and forced a cough out of her. Since he outweighed her by more than eighty pounds, his arms swallowed her until she nearly disappeared inside him.

Garrett surveyed the damage, looking from the overturned furniture and around to the lump on the floor. "Meredith, is that you?"

Jeremy stood up, surprised his legs held him, and helped Meredith to her feet. The grip on her gun didn't ease, but he understood. It would take a long time to calm the energy pounding through her. The adrenaline would eventually wane, but the memory of the bloodbath would take longer.

Meredith slid her non-weapon-toting hand against Jeremy's chest and grabbed his shirt in a hold that almost shredded it before turning to Garrett. "I finally met your brother. You know, the one you forgot to mention."

Never letting Sara go, Garrett stared at his tenant, then at Jeremy's hold on her. "I can see that."

Pax popped up next to Garrett, rising out of the haze. He sent Meredith a huge smile. "Thanks for calling me."

Jeremy wrapped an arm around her shoulders and stared down into her huge eyes. "You called him?"

She blinked until the shock decreased. "Right before we got here and I gave your phone back. Didn't you?"

"Yeah, right after that but—"

Pax stood to the side and motioned for everyone to head down the stairs in front of him. "I got Meredith's SOS first."

"We all called Pax. I got him right after the building alarm sounded on my cell." Garrett tightened his hold, then eased Sara away from him. "But we can talk about this later. Right now we need to get out of here before this place comes down."

No one said anything as they jogged down the steps and ran out into the night. The fresh air smacked into

Jeremy, pushing out the smoke-filled crud in his lungs. His coughing fit started a second later. He wasn't alone. Meredith and Sara drew in large breaths, then doubled over as their bodies shook.

Jeremy glanced at his brother through watery, smoke-filled eyes. "Where have you been?"

"I'll explain later. We need to get out of here before the authorities arrive."

Sara stood up, looking far taller than her not-quite five-foot-three frame. With a flushed face and her hands balled into fists on her hips, she stood right in front of Garrett with soot streaking her face and her singed T-shirt.

"Did you say you were worried about the authorities?" She jabbed him in the chest with a finger. "That's your big concern?"

The group fell silent. Except for the last crackle of the fire and creaky groans as the building shifted on its burning supports, nothing moved and no one breathed.

Garrett wiped a hand through his hair. "I just want—"

"You should be afraid of me," Sara nearly shouted.

Shock buzzed through Jeremy. He saw it mirrored in Garrett's eyes. The wedding-dress saleswoman who always had an encouraging word and sweet smile for everyone looked ready to explode. And Garrett was the intended target.

His eyebrows came together in a frown. "What's the matter with you?"

"You dumped me."

The final pieces fell into place for Jeremy. He shook his head. "Garrett, man. What were you thinking?"

Garrett scowled at all of them but saved his darkest look for Sara. "This isn't the time to talk about this."

Not that she even noticed. "Next time you leave a woman with some big speech about it being the right thing, don't drag her back into your life and almost get her killed."

"I tried to warn you."

"Save it." Then calm, never-cause-a-scene Sara pulled back her hand and slapped Garrett across the face.

# Chapter Nine

Andrew filled the doorway one second after knocking on Ellis's office door. "You wanted to see me, sir."

Ellis picked up the stack of files on the far left corner of his desk and dumped them in his briefcase. Those he could take. Others had to stay locked in his office for security reasons. "Darren Mitchell appears clean."

"He has an alibi?"

"I knew we would be able to account for his whereabouts since we're having him watched every second." Ellis removed his computer hard drive and put it in the safe under his desk. "No, the problem is that his records are clean. No telephone calls or unusual bank activity. The tail that's been on him says nothing unusual has happened. No guests and no activity."

When silence bounced back at him, Ellis glanced up. Andrew stood in the same spot, not moving and seemingly not breathing. "Something wrong?"

"We have someone watching Darren in addition to the electronic surveillance?"

"The man is accused of using his government position to collect money from foreign military leaders. Yes, we're watching him. If I had my way, he'd be in prison on espionage charges." Ellis shut his briefcase and leaned his palms against it. "Fortunately for him, there are those in the higher levels of government who would rather the public not know about intelligence officers on the take. Scandals like that don't exactly make people feel safer on their summer vacations."

Ellis took a second to observe his assistant. As usual, the younger man's voice vibrated with a thin layer of fear. Ellis didn't have a problem with that. Newer employees, especially those still in their probationary period, should twist and worry. It was a rite of passage of sorts.

But this was something else. Something that made the younger man's lip twitch and had him shifting his balance from foot to foot.

That settled one issue. Ellis would have company on this trip. If Andrew had something as mundane as woman troubles, time away would resolve them one way or another. If he had other troubles, Ellis would wrestle the facts out of him before the plane touched down on the West Coast. He didn't get the job with the big title by going to college with the right people. He'd worked his way up the ranks and could collect information as well as any of his operatives.

Ellis kicked the safe shut with his foot and picked up his briefcase. "Ready?"

Andrew's gaze went to the clock on the credenza. "For what? What are you doing at this time of night?"

"Leaving, and so are you."

"Excuse me?"

Andrew had gone almost two minutes without saying the phrase. Ellis figured that was a record. "We're heading to San Diego to intervene on the Hill situation."

Andrew's face fell. "I didn't realize we do that. Not a man of your position."

Ellis understood the confusion. His office oversaw operations. He didn't race across the country to check in with operatives. They functioned independently and he ruled from a distance.

But this situation was different. Something was very wrong and Ellis was not about to let some field office or an underling in a mall-store cheap suit call the shots. "We do when our best operative vanishes and someone burns his house to the ground."

Andrew started nodding and couldn't seem to stop. "I can take care of your calls and—"

"You're coming with me."

"But, sir—"

"This discussion is over." Yeah, the young man had something on his mind. Ellis vowed to wrangle the particulars out of his assistant by the top of the next hour. "You asked for field experience."

The area around Andrew's mouth turned green. "Once I'm trained. Not now."

"This will be the on-the-job kind of training."

"There's no way we can catch a flight this late."

"We're not flying commercial. This is agency business."

"But I—"

*Enough.* Ellis had listened to one more complaint than usual. "No arguments. Get packed or you go with whatever is on you and that's it."

BACK AT THE motel, Meredith stood on the small front patio and leaned back against the door to room fifteen. "What was that about with Sara?"

No one had said a thing after the verbal explosion at the safe house. Meredith didn't know the details, but hiding a girlfriend and keeping her from the pretty house in Coronado struck her as a bad choice. But she'd only heard one side and Garrett seemed reluctant to say anything at all.

After the smack-heard-around-San Diego, no one said a word. They'd filed into SUVs as Garrett walked around with his mouth dropped open. Not that Meredith had a great deal of sympathy. All the secrets and lies stacked up. Add in a firefight and actual fire and a woman could get testy. As far as Meredith was concerned, Sara had her complete support.

Jeremy sat on the porch railing across from Meredith and stretched his feet until his legs straddled hers. "Sounds like my brother lost his mind and left her."

"The slap was a surprise." The memory of Sara getting up on tiptoes to let Garrett have it would stay with Meredith for a long time. She knew how it felt to lose every last ounce of control. Having an audience only added to the embarrassment.

She liked Garrett, but he'd treated Sara pretty poorly. Took her for granted and hid things from her. Important things. Still, Sara's reaction struck Meredith as out of character. Sara didn't seem the whipped-into-a-frenzy type. Quiet, like the kind of woman men rushed to protect and coddle, yes. The prizefighter underbelly came out of nowhere.

"I've never seen her kill a fly," Jeremy said, shaking his head and *hmpfing* as he did.

"Unlike me." Meredith looked down at her hands, turned them over and watched them shake.

She'd waited for the guilt of taking a human life to rush through her but the pain never came. She knew the reality of choosing her life over theirs. She imagined the horror if she'd fired too late and Jeremy had been the one facedown, bleeding into the floor.

Looking at all the angles and her long list of sins, all she felt was numb. A vast road of nothingness.

Jeremy shifted until their feet touched. "I don't have

any complaints about you, but I do admit to judging you as the sweet type until I saw you go into commando mode."

"That had a boys-don't-make-passes-at-girls-who-wear-glasses ring to it."

"Maybe I should stop talking."

They could sit in comfortable silence, but she wanted to hear the soft rumble of his voice. It soothed out all the jagged edges inside her. "My point being, I can't figure out if 'sweet' is meant as a compliment or if the commando part was what impressed you."

The wide-eyed look of pure male panic subsided. "The mix of both. I like your tough side and your very womanly side."

She liked both sides, too. "I can live with that."

"That's a relief."

"A smart woman knows when sweetness is the wrong tactic. She fights when she doesn't have a choice." Acquiescence sounded noble and often took on the characteristics of peace, but there were times a person needed to fight.

Jeremy closed in on her without moving. Stale smoke clung to his clothes and his hair, bathing him in an acid cologne. He'd washed the soot off but a tiny patch still covered his right cheek near his hairline.

"Who taught you that lesson?" he asked.

The history shaped everything but no longer meant anything. "Doesn't matter."

"It does to me."

"Why?"

He pushed off the railing and moved to stand in front of her, her legs trapped between his. "I'm wondering who I have to beat the crap out of on your behalf once we settle whatever is going on around here."

A laugh burst to life inside her, but she pushed the infectious happiness down deep and concentrated on the conversation. "You barely know me."

"Yet the idea of someone hurting you makes me crazed." Jeremy trailed the backs of his fingers against her cheek. "I wonder why that is."

"Must be the government agent thing."

"You know it's more than that, right?"

She rubbed the soot off his face with her thumb. "Adrenaline rush."

He dipped his head and brushed his nose against hers. His mouth hovered at the corner of hers as his breath skipped across her cheek. "Try again."

When his lips replaced his breath, her brain fizzled. "An ex-boyfriend."

Jeremy pulled back, his gaze searching hers. "What?"

"The violence. I was young. He was a loser, probably still is." Meredith rested her palms against Jeremy's chest and leaned in just a little. "The day he pushed me down a flight of stairs was a wake-up call. I lay there, waiting until he left the house to 'clear his head' and then I got ready."

At the mention of the abuse the skin around Jeremy's mouth pulled tight. He didn't show any other reaction except for a subtle stiffness in his shoulders. "For what exactly?"

"I greeted him with my bags packed and a loaded gun. I'd been taking lessons, shooting and self-protection."

Jeremy's hands moved to her upper arms. The hold stayed loose, as if letting her know that she could bolt at any time and he would respect her decision. "Sounds dangerous."

"No, staying was dangerous. It was the only time he got physical, but the emotional battering wore me down to the point where I didn't see it coming."

Jeremy bit his bottom lip then let it go. "Please don't defend him."

"I wasn't." Was she?

"You know any violence is unconscionable, right? Name-calling or whatever he did to you, same thing. Not your fault and not okay. The guy doesn't get a pass for only shoving you one time."

"Sounds like you've had some experience with this."

"No." He rubbed circles over her skin with his thumbs. "We were raised by a single mom who lectured us about the way a man should treat a woman. When she died she asked only that we be decent men when we grew up."

The simple words explained so much. Meredith's heart ached for him, for the young man who lost his anchor. "How old were you?"

"Seventeen. Breast cancer."

"I'm so sorry."

"Did you have to shoot this guy?"

She figured he'd shared enough and it was her turn. "Let's say I fired a warning shot."

All the tension left Jeremy's face as a smile crept across his lips. "Into what part of him?"

"Wondered if you'd figure that out." She basked in the acceptance. Jeremy didn't judge or shrink away from the details. If anything, the idea of her defending herself relaxed him. "His foot. I figured he wouldn't run after me that way."

"I would have aimed a little higher, but still effective."

"It was tempting." Part of her still couldn't believe she'd worked up the courage to pull the trigger. It took her another year to find the nerve to tell her parents the truth about the relationship. They were close, but having them know, the idea of giving them a peek into what her daily life had become, made her stomach roll.

All the "he was such a nice boy" conversations stopped after that. Her father threatened revenge. Her mother baked five apple pies. The balance of the parent–daughter relationship evened out again, but Meredith waited every holiday for the pitying looks and concerned whispers about how she was doing and what they could do to help.

Jeremy put his hand under her chin with the barest of pressure. "One more favor. Please tell me you're not still carrying a torch for this dumbass."

"It was six years ago. The feelings are long gone. He killed most of them when he insisted I fell down the steps and he tried to catch me." The physical bruises had healed, but welts no one could see, the ones formed from the never-ending list of her failings, still came back and whapped her now and then.

"Did this man kill everything inside you?"

"I don't know what that means." But she did. The heat was right there in Jeremy's eyes, banked but still burning.

Attraction hit her in rare instances, most of them cloaked in safety, like with the guy behind the coffee counter who barely knew her name and the teacher at her school who never showed any sign of interest. But those old dreams of a normal life with a husband she loved and trusted came rushing back now and then.

She went out. She tried. She just hated the games and the silliness, and at the first sign of bullying behavior she bolted. That left her with a long list of first dates but a much shorter record of second ones.

Violence terrified her and she'd spent hours analyzing behavior and worrying if she'd missed obvious signs. Big men and military men were on her no-go list. The mix of strength and weapons sent her head spinning with fear.

Then Garrett walked into her life. Instead of panicking over his combination of mystery and protectiveness, she enjoyed it.

Looking now at Jeremy, she felt something different. One second spent touring those broad shoulders and her blood heated in her veins and her mouth went dry. She wanted to talk and get to know him, even as her brain screamed at her to hide until he sneaked out of town again.

He cupped her cheek and ran a thumb over her suddenly dry lips. "Do you really not understand the question?"

"I'm not into big men."

He leaned his forehead against hers. "Do you know how tempting it is to make a tasteless joke right now?"

The laughter bubbled up from her chest. This time she didn't try to stop it. She let the amusement flow through her and wipe out some of the horror of the day.

She pressed a hand to her mouth and wrestled with her control. "You'd think I'd know better since I'm usually with a group of little boys all day. They say things that would make their parents cry."

"Boys can be gross."

"But cute." She gave in to the urge to trail her hand across his chest. Firm dips and bulges pressed against her palm. "Especially the grown-up ones."

"Maybe I should get a tip or two from your students."

"You're doing fine."

"That's good because unless you tell me no, I'm going to kiss you. Long and deep, hot and a bit naughty." He shifted his hands to her hips and pulled her close until his body pressed against hers.

"Jeremy, I—"

"I'll stop before we go too far because it's been a pretty

long and not-so-great day, but believe me when I say I won't want to pull back."

"Still dealing with that surge of adrenaline?"

"Don't give the credit to the danger high. It's been an hour. The night is dark and you're sexy, and if you wiggle like that one more time I'm throwing you over my shoulder and carrying you into that room." He nodded in the general direction of the door. "And I won't care about my bad timing until tomorrow."

Even his words made her insides all jumpy, as if her skin no longer fit right and her clothes were too tight. "You're not scaring me."

"Really? This—" he waved his hand between them "—scares the crap out of me."

Then his mouth was on hers. No nibbling or hesitation. His lips fit over hers, caressing and coaxing until his tongue swept inside and his hand plunged into her hair. The heat enveloped her as the firm touch of him from head to knees sent her heart into a thudding beat.

She wrapped her arms around his neck and held on as he lifted her a little. All those boring dates and wasted minutes dropped away. This was about want and need, about the intoxicating feel of his firm body next to hers. About this perfect moment at the end of the most imperfect day.

The warmth wrapping around her. The clasp of his hands. The brush of his skin against hers. It all collided in an energy-sucking kiss that made her knees buckle. Everything from his scent to his hold would haunt her dreams.

He lifted his head, but not before treating her to one more kiss. "Did I really say I'd stop tonight?"

"You did."

"Shows what an idiot I am."

Her sneakers hit the floor but her heart floated about two feet above her. "In your defense, it sounded like a good idea at the time."

"Go inside before I forget my training and lose control."

His kisses made her dizzy. The force of her weakness for him snapped her back to life. "That would be a bad thing, right?"

His exhalation blew by her. "The timing is wrong."

"Always the gentleman."

"There's nothing proper about what I'm thinking about right now." He backed up, putting a foot between them that may as well have been a mile. "Besides that, I need to go torture my brother."

"It's my turn after you."

"I'll let him know he might have another slap in his future. And, Meredith?"

"Yeah?"

Jeremy caught her around the waist and pulled her in for a long, drawing kiss. The kind that had good girls thinking nasty thoughts.

Her vision blurred when she raised her head again. "Uh-huh."

He shot her a knee-buckling wink. "Good night."

## Chapter Ten

Bruce traced his finger over the carvings in the table-top. The graffiti consisted of a mash-up of profanity and empty declarations of love. Not very inventive, and barely interesting as a form of entertainment since he didn't have time for either of those pastimes. Didn't have time for prison, conference rooms or an overpaid lawyer either.

The overpaid professional in question smoothed his hand over his jacket lapel as he practiced his bored blank stare. "Why did you call me back here tonight?"

Bruce focused on a drawing of a tiny man with not so tiny private parts and tried to figure out why the other prisoners would use perfectly sharp weapons for such a stupid task as scratching figures and words in metal. And the pledges of love to women. He'd bet those same women had landed most of the men in there.

The last woman he let in his bed turned out to be a disloyal whore. Thanks to him she wouldn't ruin another man's life.

"I need to get a message to someone," he said.

"You said this was an emergency. It's after visiting hours. Do you have any idea how many favors I had to call in to make this happen?"

"I don't care." He looked up then, catching the dripping disdain on Stephen's face right before he hid it.

"This is an abusive waste of my valuable time." The lawyer stood up, swaying as he did thanks to the stomach puffing over his belt. If his puffy stomach grew any bigger, he'd have to lower his waistband to his feet. "I have other clients."

"Sit."

Stephen fell back into his chair. "I'm listening."

Amazing how one word said in the perfect tone got the job done every time. Bruce learned that lesson from his father. The only worthwhile thing the man ever passed on.

"I am your priority, Stephen, and I expect to be treated as such." Bruce held up a finger when the other man started to open his mouth. "When I call, you come here. That is the rule from now on, Stephen. Do you understand?"

The other man clenched the arms of his chair. "How dare—"

"Cleary, you don't. I'll try again." Looked like it was time for a serious reality check. Bruce had nothing but time, and making threats came to him as easily as breathing. "You will do as I say or your career will end."

"What is that supposed to mean?"

"I think you know." Bruce leaned back in his chair, enjoying the way Stephen gulped in air and fidgeted in his seat. "Back to the topic of my message."

Stephen's big-lawyer sputtering and red-faced rage died down. "This is moot. All of your mail except specific correspondence with me that could be privileged is reviewed. That's one of the rules around here."

"Which is why I'm coming to you with this request."

"I have no intention of smuggling notes out of here for you. This isn't fifth grade and I am not about to lose my law license over something so obvious to the guards."

For a smart man with a bunch of fancy degrees, Stephen sure wasn't getting the point. Proved that all that money and growing up with servants didn't buy street smarts.

Bruce decided to be a bit less subtle. He wasn't accustomed to watching his words anyway. "You will do as I say."

"You're not listening."

"You don't seem to understand your position here."

"You're the one in prison." Stephen smiled as he dropped that fact.

"You think a few bars on the window stopped my business? All this talk of drug tunnels and marijuana, and you've missed the bigger picture."

"Which is?"

Bruce let the legs of his chair fall to the floor with a thwap. He slapped his hands against the table, satisfied when Stephen jumped in reaction. "I have a network of allies and business associates. I can't control all of their actions, but I do find their loyalty to me very comforting."

Stephen's face fell flat. All the light and color seeped out of him. "Are you threatening me?"

"Merely making a statement. After all, our relationship only works when we can be honest with each other, right?" Bruce figured he had waited long enough. Time to stop this nonsense where Stephen thought he had the upper hand. He'd see who was in charge. "I'm sure your son would agree. Conrad is his name, isn't it?"

If possible, Stephen turned even paler. "He's not involved in my business. He's just a kid."

"And a smart one. How is he doing at Brown?"

Bruce was enjoying the performance now. Watching Stephen shift in his seat and loosen his tie made Bruce wish he'd pulled this stunt earlier. Every part of him vibrated with the thrill of taking a bloated hypocrite down.

Sure, Stephen would accept his money while insisting he valued the system. He'd bask in the glory of his amazing litigation skills but insist they never share a meal. It was garbage. Bruce knew the truth. They were the same. They shared a common goal—make money, build the business, succeed.

"How did you know about my son?" The question came out as a whispered plea.

"I know everything, Stephen. That's what you seem to forget."

"But I—"

"I hear Archibald House is nice. That roommate of his, though." Bruce shook his head as he made a *tsk-tsk* sound. "Lots of alcohol and a C in chemistry. You need to be careful with that young man. I'd hate to see Conrad get sucked into that lifestyle. He could be in the wrong place at the wrong time and who knows what would happen."

Rage poured out of Stephen. "What do you want?"

"As I said, I need to get a message to a business associate."

"Is he in Arizona?"

"He's on assignment in San Diego at the moment, and I'm depending on you to help us keep in touch. It's imperative right now that I communicate with him."

Flustered, his hands waving as he dumped his briefcase back on the table, Stephen gritted his teeth as he talked. "I can put him on your guest list."

The more out of control the lawyer got, the more at ease Bruce felt. This was a balance of power he could appreciate. "My associate isn't in a position to come in and out of here. He's needed in California."

"For what?"

"Do you really want to know?"

Stephen shook his head. "What's his name?"

"You don't need to know that either. I'll give you all the information you require to get the job done."

"And then?"

*Jeremy Hill will die.*

Bruce smiled. "I'll let you know."

STANDING IN THE motel bathroom, Sara slipped the oversize T-shirt over her head and let it fall to her knees. Joel had dropped off the change of clothes and a few toiletries a few hours ago. Despite the fact that it was nearly two in the morning, she still couldn't sleep. Her nerves jumped from all the excitement and fear swirling inside her.

Running into Garrett's open arms the second after his face appeared above the stairs had been pure instinct. She'd seen the firm jaw and those intense blue eyes and her heart had melted. The terror of the moments before, lying in the back behind a bed with her arms over her ears as she prayed for a miracle, hammered at her anger toward him. When what she thought was the end had come, she'd wanted him with a desperation that stunned her.

Now, hours later, she wasn't sure she even wanted to see him. Not that he'd honored her concerns. No. When she'd asked him to get his own room he'd dumped his bag on her bed and told her he'd be back after the men talked strategy.

Now he was back, and the time to deal with him, with them, and all that had passed between them, had come.

Her hand curled around the doorknob and she stopped. On the other side of the bathroom door stood the one man who both lit a fire of need in her belly and filled her with a brain-chilling fury.

He'd walked out on her.

The door rattled on its hinges as the pounding started. "Sara? What's taking so long in there?"

Working up her nerve while clamping a lid on her fury had taken longer than she'd expected. Night had fully fallen and the abandoned area around the motel added to the desolated feel. They rode only a short time outside of downtown San Diego, but this place felt hours away. No street lights. No other cars. Just the Hill brothers, Garrett's team and a woman named Meredith.

Just thinking about the other woman put a flame to Sara's already sparking anger. "Why don't you go to your new girlfriend's room?"

Something thudded against the door, likely his hand. "That's you. You're the only woman I have in my life and I'm having a difficult enough time dealing with you."

He acted like she was to blame. The idiot. "You won't have to worry about that anymore."

"I will break this door down if you don't—"

She threw it open and his weight against the wood pulled him into the bathroom. "What, Garrett? Tell me."

His mouth snapped shut.

Seeing the spooked expression cross his face, the wide-eyed confusion she'd never seen before, built a new wall of strength inside her. "Well?"

"I need to talk with you."

She pushed passed him into the bedroom. She stopped when her knees hit the bed because she realized she didn't have anywhere else to go. No way was she wandering around outside alone. She'd had enough excitement for one evening. For a lifetime, actually.

She was the assistant manager at a bridal store. Brides could be strange and difficult but none of them tried to shoot her.

"You said everything a few weeks ago, or should I recap for you?"

He frowned down at her as his hands hit his hips. "What's gotten into you?"

She understood the root of his confusion. Their relationship had bumped along with her accepting and him running here and there with little to no notice. She'd spent a lot of nights and weekends alone. She'd gone weeks without seeing him and barely hearing from him.

She rarely complained. She accepted, thinking it would all be fine once they got married.

Seeing him get down on one knee and propose had been the best day of her life. The night under the stars, the roaring waves as they'd hit the beach and the sand that seeped between her toes. In an airy white dress, she'd felt free and so loved.

Then he'd started talking about getting the wedding over so he could protect her better. The words, his attitude, sucked all the romance out of what should have been the sighing early days of their engagement.

"You turned me into this," she whispered in a voice filled with all the anguish stirring inside her.

"The fire and gunfire in the safe house was my fault. I take responsibility for that."

"I'm talking about when I didn't agree to stand in the living room and let some stranger marry us on a random Tuesday night. The next day you told me we needed to rethink our relationship."

"We're back to that? Look, I wasn't thinking straight. I was upset."

"That made two of us."

"True, but—"

"Then you left town." Tension twirled and twisted in her brain until the spring popped loose. "And now I meet Meredith."

"Right, I can explain about that." He reached for her.

Sara shrugged away from him. The thought of his hands on her right now made her murderous. "Who is she?"

"It's not what you think."

"I think you're a jerk."

He held his hands in front of him as if he knew the chance of being slapped again was pretty good. "Maybe, but not for the reason you're assuming."

"I'm waiting."

"She rented an apartment from me."

The words lay there. Sara turned them over in her mind and still couldn't make sense of them.

"What are you talking about?" The air hiccuped in her lungs and refused to come out. "Wait a second. You have another place?"

"A house in Coronado."

The force of his betrayal nearly doubled her over. "Were you planning to tell me before we got married?"

"Of course."

The snide tone had her back teeth slamming together. "Don't say it like that. You don't get to be angry. Not when you lived with another woman behind my back."

"It wasn't like that."

Sara wrapped her arms around her stomach and pressed as tight as she could. She knew if she let go her insides would spill onto the floor. Her body rocked as the words poured out of her in a deflated rush. "I was so stupid. I actually thought this was a cold-feet issue. That you'd take some time and get over it."

He touched her elbow and moved in front of her. "I asked you to elope."

"You wanted to rush everything until it meant nothing. And all the time you had this other woman."

"Never. I wouldn't cheat. You know that." He held her

upper arms, bringing her in close. "Meredith rented the upstairs apartment, and thanks to me she lost everything when the house blew up."

"Don't ask me to feel sorry for her."

"She's as innocent as you are, Sara. Don't hate her."

He had the wrong target. Interesting how a smart man could so easily miss the obvious. "Right now I hate you."

But she didn't. That was the terrible secret that made her doubt her brainpower. Despite all the hurt and pain, all the fear and lies, she loved him with every breath.

"I don't think you do." He laid a hand against her heart.

It beat even harder through her skin. She wanted to lean in, to borrow his heat and his strength. Instead she dug deep into her reserves and found the will to fight back.

"Find another room." She pushed his hand away.

"No."

His quick response stunned her. It took a few seconds to form the right sentence in response. "Don't add another sin to your list."

"I won't touch you until you ask me, and you will ask, but I won't leave you unprotected either." His hands dropped to his sides.

During their two years together she thought she'd seen every step on his range of emotions. For a flash, just a second, she witnessed something new. His skin stretched and his eyes dulled. Then his features went blank. No warmth, no anger, nothing.

"How do you do that?" she asked.

"What?"

"Compartmentalize. Turn your feelings off and shut down until you're nothing more than a machine." He pushed her away without even knowing it. Every shove broke off something inside her until she didn't know if she could put the pieces back together again.

"It's my job."

That was the company line. She knew what he did and accepted the danger. She just hated what the emotional detachment did to him. "You're more than your work."

He ran his fingertips down her cheek. "Only when I'm with you."

Then he walked out the door.

## Chapter Eleven

Jeremy stood at the end of the building and watched Garrett pace around outside Sara's room. He'd stop and hold his hand up to the doorknob, then let it drop again. After the sixth time he swiped his hand through his hair, Jeremy took pity on him.

"It's getting close to three. You should get some sleep." His footsteps echoed against the wood as he walked.

Garrett didn't turn around or act surprised. With his training he sensed when someone got too close or conducted surveillance on him. "You're not going to ask?"

Jeremy groaned as he dropped down on the step and spun a water bottle between his palms. "About what you're doing with Meredith and what happened with Sara? Yeah, I want to know but I figure you'll tell me when you're ready."

"I screwed up." Garrett dropped down beside him.

"Obviously."

Garrett laughed, his mouth turning into something other than a frown for the first time since he'd stormed into the safe house. "They don't teach you about dealing with women in DIA training."

"You mean someone knows that secret? Man, they should share with all us other clueless men out here."

Garrett shook his head. "I just wanted to get married

fast so Sara would be protected if something happened to me. She'd get the benefits and cover if she needed it. But she didn't understand."

Jeremy winced. "Being her bodyguard wasn't the only reason you wanted to get married, was it?"

"Huh?"

"Never mind. So, you left." He balanced his elbows on his knees and linked his fingers together in front of him. "Honestly, I'm surprised. That's really not your style."

"I got ticked off and needed some time away." Garrett shook his head as he spread his legs out in front of him. "Then I figured out Darren Mitchell, this guy on another team, was playing around with operation funds and I had to set up a sting. Took me weeks to build the evidence. It's why I haven't been in touch with you either."

"You get him?"

He nodded. "Which is probably why we're under attack now."

While Jeremy studied the angles, it sounded like Garrett had narrowed the suspect pool to one. "This Darren guy have these kind of connections?"

"I didn't think so, but the timing fits. Without me the case gets shaky. He has all the incentive in the world to take me out."

"We both have a lot of enemies."

"Sure feels that way." Garrett gave him eye contact for the first time. "Heard you got stabbed. You okay?"

All the stretching and pulling had opened the wound again and now it ached. Jeremy didn't realize it, hadn't even felt it until he got back to the motel. Pax had restitched it and threatened him with an infection if he messed up again.

Jeremy had ducked into a bathroom to keep Meredith from seeing the bloodstain. She liked to touch and nurse and he liked her soft caresses, but right now he needed some space between them.

The phone vibrated in Jeremy's back pocket. He slipped it out at the same time Garrett reached for his. The screens clicked on at the same time. The image of the yard flicked on the screen. Someone had tripped the far motion sensors.

"You seeing this?" he asked Garrett.

"Not good."

The press of a button later, Jeremy saw a sea of green dots converging on the motel. "They're coming in bunches now."

Garrett jumped to his feet and unscrewed the light bulb above his head. They'd disabled the others outside, so without this one the motel plunged into darkness. "We've got lots of company this round."

"Looks like at least eight." This team moved with a military-like precision, organized and smart. They didn't race up the middle or telegraph their position. "You still thinking Darren is at the bottom of all this?"

"Let's keep one of these men alive and we'll be able to ask him who's paying him for his dirty work."

Jeremy knocked on the doors at the ends of the L-shaped building. Joel, Pax and Davis hit their doorways, armed and wearing vests. If they'd been resting, it sure didn't show. They stood wide-eyed and ready for battle.

"How many do we have out there?" Pax asked.

"Enough to worry about." Garrett knocked on Sara's door but didn't get a response. "We need protection on the women and shooters ready to fire at any movement. If those men get up to the building, this scene could get really ugly."

"And we have innocents," Davis said.

"Exactly. Pax and Davis, take the left. Use the roof. Joel, go with Garrett and fan out in front." Jeremy pointed as he issued the orders. "If you can keep them from getting to the motel, all the better."

"Done." Pax took off and motioned for Davis to follow.

"I'll guard the ladies." Jeremy's voice never lifted past a whisper even though rough demands shouted in his brain.

"Let me talk to Sara first. She's still spooked by the last round." Garrett touched the doorknob.

Jeremy put a hand up to stop him. "I'll handle it. You get in position."

Indecision battled in every line of Garrett's face. He stared at the door then out into the dark and back again.

Jeremy knew they couldn't afford the extra time. "I'll take care of her, man. Just go."

Jeremy didn't give his brother a choice. He knocked one more time then pushed his way in. He glanced at the bed expecting to see a lump, but only spied rumpled pillows.

"How bad is it?"

His gaze zoomed to the corner at the sound of Sara's soft voice. She stood half bent over, holding her sweats and stood still enough to blend into the gaudy wallpaper.

Jeremy's heart tumbled. He'd always loved Sara. Not for him, but for Garrett. Jeremy had once worried she was too soft and sweet for his hard brother. But she could make Garrett smile just by walking into the room. She cooked for them, coddled them and had Garrett spinning. Jeremy knew if his brother would stop throwing up barriers, he'd have a happy life with Sara.

So, Jeremy knew he owed it to her to tell the truth. "There are men coming."

"Where's Garrett?"

"Watching over the front and finalizing the plan."

"You mean he's sacrificing himself. He'll figure out some near-suicidal way to end this so only he gets hurt."

"I'm not going to let that happen."

"Do you get a say? I don't."

Jeremy didn't have time to fix his brother's bad choices. But he didn't want her to go into another dangerous situation thinking Garrett no longer cared. "The rescuer thing is his messed up way of telling you he loves you. Words aren't his strength. His day job requires him to use his fists to make his point. Changing tactics in his private life has been…"

"A struggle?"

"And that's a nice way of putting it."

"For the record, if he gets hurt I'm going to strangle him."

The pushy save-him-or-else attitude had to be a good sign for Garrett's wooing campaign. At least Jeremy hoped that was true.

"If it comes to him deciding to go out in a blaze of glory, I'll stop it. Then I'll hold him down for you while you beat some sense into him."

"I can live with that."

Jeremy winked at her and held out a hand. "We have to go."

He pulled her behind him until they stood in front of room fifteen. A quick glance behind him told him that the team was in place. He couldn't see anyone. If he hadn't known this was an armed camp, he would have assumed it was an abandoned motel, which was exactly what everyone should think.

Meredith opened the door before he could knock. "What is it?"

He took in her sweatpants and slim T-shirt. She'd already put her sneakers on and had a gun in her hand. The woman didn't back down from a fight.

He liked her spirit. "I thought you'd be asleep."

"Something woke me up. A weird sensation." She looked around him into the darkness beyond. "What's happening that everyone's up and moving?"

"A second strike. More men are coming." Sara's voice stayed even as she delivered the horrifying message.

Meredith blinked. "But you said this was off the grid, that the highway no longer came through here."

The same questions had been floating through his mind. Their safe houses had been compromised. The reasons for that sort of system-wide malfunction were few. "I know."

"Then how did anyone find us?" Meredith asked. Her voice held a yearning and confusion he hadn't heard before.

"Good question."

And there was only one answer—a mole.

But he couldn't take that issue on along with everything else he had to juggle. As it was, every time he moved a thousand tiny swords rammed into his side. The stitches pulled and the area pulsed with pain. The only course was to ignore it, pretend everything was fine.

He glanced at the image on his phone and saw the green dots fanning out, coming at the motel in an arc. The spray of bullets would start any minute. His people had the advantage, but a stray bullet could kill any of them.

He glanced at Meredith. Could kill her. The thought sent a chill shooting through him.

"Get back in the room. Pax is above us."

"What if the bad guys circle this place?" Sara asked.

They were dead. It was that simple. "Not going to happen."

Gunfire burst through the quiet night.

"Get down!" He grabbed them both and crowded them against the bathroom wall. "Get in there and close the door. There's no window, so only open this door for me or Garrett. And don't move."

Before Meredith could argue, he scooted across the room to the small window by the door. From his position on the ground he could peek over the sill and see outside.

Shadows moved off to his left. Shots echoed all around him until it was impossible to tell who was shooting and who was under fire. One man went down. The trees behind him rustled, then another shooter popped out, this one aiming for the roof and unloading.

Jeremy ducked with his hands over his head as ceiling tiles fell to the bed and floor. The glass above his head shattered and shards rained down on his back.

At the sound of crunching, he looked up to see Meredith crouching beside him. "What are you doing?"

"Making sure you weren't cut into a million pieces." She grabbed a pillow off the edge of the bed and used it to brush the sharp slivers off him and away from his knees.

The booming came from all sides. That qualified as a very bad sign. "Sounds like someone got through."

"What?" she shouted over the steady beat of gunfire.

He heard the thunder of footsteps. A peek out the hole in the wall showed a man sneaking up the side of the building. He'd somehow gotten through the defenses Joel and Garrett had set up. Jeremy refused to let his mind go there. His brother was fine. They were all fine, but they had to end this.

Pivoting on the ball of his foot, Jeremy put the barrel out the window and shot at the closest intruder. He fell, then scrambled for the bushes just out of sight.

If he got around back, protection would become impossible. Watching 360 degrees in the pitch dark required special equipment that they just didn't have.

Meredith snapped her fingers in front of his face. "How many are left?"

He looked at the screen. "I have five. From the positions, two of the figures should be Joel and Garrett."

"Anyone close?"

"One is on top of us." He pulled her close and whispered directly into her ear. "I'm going out there."

Meredith grabbed his arm. "Please stay with me."

At the plea he almost relented. For once he welcomed the darkness and his inability to read her expression. "You're my cover."

After a brief hesitation, she nodded, smacking the top of her head against his chin. "What do I do?"

"Fire off to the right." He tapped on the bottom of her gun until she raised it. "Up high so you don't hit me. The plan is to keep this attacker from unloading on me while I track him down."

She'd already gotten in position. "I'm ready."

He wanted to say something, to at least kiss her, but he slipped out the door instead. Bent low, he eased around the door and raised his gun. Glass littered the ground and he placed careful footsteps to keep from smashing the shards under his feet. Any noise could give him away.

He glanced at the phone one last time. Another dot not moving and slowly changing color, which could only mean one thing. Someone got hit. He took a second to hope the body was one of theirs, not his.

His target hovered nearby. He jumped when Meredith stared firing behind him. The rustle off to the side of the porch gave the attacker's precise position away.

Jeremy dived, sliding down the porch on his stomach. When his shoulder slipped off the wood and into the air, he shifted and fired right into the figure looming over him.

The guy went down with a muffled yell. He rolled to the grass and came to a stop on his stomach. Jeremy slithered onto the ground after him. His eyes had adjusted to the black night, but seeing the dark metal of the attacker's gun proved difficult.

Meredith kept shooting. He turned to tell her to stop, to get a half second of quiet, when the man on the ground reared up. He rolled to his side and turned with a gun already in his hand.

It happened in a flash. Jeremy saw the weapon and judged the distance. He lifted his own gun, but he knew the timing was all wrong. He shifted and prayed he'd be in time.

With one last ear-splitting shot, the attacker's head fell back to the ground as his hands splayed to the side. In the slow-motion haze following the shooting, Jeremy saw shoes and heard yelling. When he looked up, Joel stood over his shoulder with his gun still up and ready. Meredith hovered behind him.

Joel slowly lowered his gun. "He was wearing a vest. I know you probably wanted to question him, but I had to shoot him in the head."

"Where did you come from?" Jeremy couldn't get the fog in his brain to clear. He knew it was a blessing. As soon as feeling returned to his body and his ears stopped ringing, the pain in his side would come screaming back.

"What?"

"You're supposed to be up front with Garrett."

Joel looked at the glass and wood chips all around his feet. "You needed me here."

The green on Jeremy's cell caught his attention. One dot moved up the lawn as two others climbed off the roof. Garrett wasn't exactly making a covert entrance. He grumbled as he undid his vest, letting the sound of Velcro rip through the now-still night.

Meredith shifted as if ready to shoot, and Jeremy was on her in seconds. He put his hand on her arm and lowered the weapon. "It's okay. He's with us."

Garrett stormed right up the path and jumped onto the porch. He didn't look at anyone, not even Sara as she hugged the doorjamb.

He stopped in front of Joel. His hands shot out and he pinned the younger man against the side of the motel. Joel's head smacked against the wall as he fought to push Garrett back.

"What the—"

Garrett pressed his forearm against Joel's throat. He gagged as he kicked out.

Jeremy stepped in to help but the black rage clouding Garrett's eyes stopped him.

"I don't—" Joel tried to talk but coughed over Garrett's forearm.

Pax and Davis didn't move. All attention centered on Garrett and his rage. His hands trembled as he grabbed Joel's collar and twisted even harder.

Garrett leaned in, his face just inches from Joel's. "You have ten minutes to tell me what the hell is going on."

# Chapter Twelve

Meredith worried Garrett had careened right over the edge. The veins in his arms popped from the force of holding Joel against the wall.

Jeremy must have had the same concern because he tried to intervene. "Garrett, man. Ease up."

When his brother's concentration remained focused, Jeremy just stood there with slumped shoulders and a mouth turned down in a frown. Desperate to lessen the unease she felt radiating off him, she leaned in and slipped her fingers through his.

She half expected Jeremy to shake her off and grab Garrett. Not that she would blame Jeremy or even be surprised. Testosterone thumped through the air. He might have to rush in and stop a fight at any minute. It would be rational if he dropped her hand and went after Garrett again. The move would sting and rub against her pride a bit, but she'd get it.

Which was why, when he grabbed on as if she were his lifeline, something burst free in her stomach. She didn't know she was nervous until he held on.

All that running, all those fears, and it turned out the one type of man she'd always vowed to avoid made her heart shudder. Life never ceased to amaze her.

"What happened?" Pax glanced at Davis then back to Garrett. "I don't get this."

With a second shove, Garrett pushed Joel's back against the wall again. "Everyone stay out of this. This is between me and him."

"It's too late for that. We're in it. All of us." Davis went from lounging against a beam to stepping right between Garrett and Joel. With his hand on top of Garrett's, Davis tried to pull the two men apart. "And last I checked we were on the same side."

Despite Davis's size and obvious strength, Garrett didn't move. He braced his legs and pushed even harder against Joel's chest. "Are we?"

Joel's eyes narrowed. "What's wrong with you?"

It was the same question playing in Meredith's mind. Probably in all of their minds. She'd seen Garrett distracted as he rushed out the door on assignments and relaxed when he nursed a beer on the porch after his return. This out of control, ready to pounce and shred a man apart with his bare hands Garrett scared her.

She glanced at Sara, expecting the other woman to be curled in a ball or crying in a corner. The judgment probably wasn't fair, but Sara didn't strike Meredith as much of a fighter. She hid and froze when she needed to run and fight. The reaction was likely what a sane person who'd never seen violence would do in similar situations, but Meredith couldn't fight off the nagging disappointment.

Lounging on her couch at night, she'd imagined the woman Garrett might find attractive. Built a model in her mind, and Sara wasn't it. She was pretty, really pretty, and had that tiny fragile frame men seemed to love. But she lacked fire. There was no heat to her.

Except right now. Sara inched closer to Garrett. Without blinking, her gaze switched from Garrett to Joel. In a matter of seconds, her cheeks puffed and her assessing gaze mimicked Garrett's.

He curled his hands around Joel's collar. "Why didn't you shoot?"

Joel sputtered. "What?"

"Garrett. Let the man have some air. He's not going anywhere and this isn't helping." Jeremy yanked Garrett's hands off Joel's shirt and put his palm out. "Joel, hand over your gun."

"No way." Joel looked to Pax. "Help me here."

"I don't need to hear from him. No guns. No misunderstandings." Jeremy let go of Meredith's hand then. He slid Joel's gun out of its holster. "I'll hold this until we're done."

He passed her the gun. The simple act delivered a huge message. The world tilted and exploded around them, but he trusted her. She hugged that knowledge close to her heart as she held on to the gun with both hands.

Davis swore as he stepped off the porch and into the yard. "This is so messed up."

"Garrett," Jeremy said. "Get to it."

"You looked at the guy heading along the right fence. You watched and tracked and then you let him go."

"I didn't—"

Garrett held up his hand. His lip curled back as he bared his teeth. "Do not deny it. I watched you."

"Garrett, please calm down." Sara tugged on his arm then.

As soon as she touched him, some of the air seeped out of him. His chest deflated as he glanced down at Sara with a look so intimate and wrecked that Meredith felt guilty seeing it.

She turned away, but not before the pleading in his eyes tore at her. When she looked up again, Jeremy was in front of her. Sturdy, dependable Jeremy. He joked. He shot. He protected. And right now he wore an unreadable expression.

If the scene between Garrett and Sara affected Jeremy, he didn't let it show. For some reason, that ripped at her just as hard as the show of love.

"You could have been killed." Garrett brushed his hand down Sara's cheek.

The window opened and Meredith had a peek at Garrett's softness. Then it slammed shut again with equal force and the shield went up. He morphed back into super soldier, to the same type of rough-around-the-edges guy as the brother who'd knocked her to the sidewalk when her house exploded.

She looked from Jeremy to Garrett. She'd thought they were different but they really weren't. For the first time she wondered just how deep their similarities ran.

"You and Meredith, all of you. All of you could have been killed before I could stop it." A harsh kick moved into Garrett's voice as he stared at Sara. "So, I want an explanation."

"You had him," Joel shouted before anyone turned back to him.

Garrett put his hands on Sara's shoulders and shifted her to his side. When he faced Joel again, all signs of the boyfriend were gone. "Since when do we make another member of the team clean up our mess? Something else was going on out there. Something in your head. I want to know what it was."

Pax threw his hands up in the air. "Joel, just tell him what he wants to know and end this."

"What do you know about it?" Joel shot back.

"I know our cover is blown here and we need to leave. You two also have to clear this up or it's going to infect everything else." With that, Pax joined his brother on the lawn. The two of them paced, tension bouncing between them as they avoided the scene on the porch.

Jeremy put a hand on Joel's shoulder. "Pax is right. I'm sure there's a simple explanation. Get to it, then we can make plans for where we go from here."

Garrett nodded. "You could have shot and run. Taken them both out and not left any opening for a counterattack."

"That would have tipped off this one and I wanted to stop him before he reached the motel." Joel pointed at the dead man only a few feet from where they all stood.

The explanation made sense to Meredith, but she didn't know the men or their field training. She saw how they acted under pressure, which was better than most men. Garrett saw something else. He kept driving, trying to make a point.

"What are you thinking here?" she asked.

"An attack on the safe house. Another on the motel." Garrett ticked off the instances on his fingers. "That's two locations no one was supposed to know about. We're the only people with access and knowledge—and Ellis."

She turned to Jeremy. "Who's Ellis?"

"Garrett's superior at DIA."

"I didn't tell him we were coming to the motel," Garrett said.

Meredith didn't get the point. From the way Sara's mouth dropped open, Meredith guessed she was lost, too. "But this Ellis guy knows about this place? Is it possible he's—"

Garrett finally spared her a glance. "Ellis is not the mole, so I'm wondering who is."

He was so sure. Meredith didn't feel equally certain. Emotion seemed to be guiding his thoughts, which was something she never dreamed she'd say about Garrett. As far as she was concerned, he—all of them, really— kept missing one very big point. That Jeremy could be the target.

"You think I betrayed the team?" Joel asked.

"You're the only one acting in a way I can't explain." Some of the heat had left Garrett's voice. He rubbed the back of his neck. "You think I want to go there?"

"Okay." Jeremy pulled Sara out of the middle of the chaos and added his body into the mix. "Look, this isn't getting us anywhere."

Pax sprinted back up the steps and handed his keys to Jeremy. "We need to move. I'm getting itchy standing out here, waiting for the next wave to hit."

"The garage," Davis called out from the lawn.

"Davis and I have a garage just south of downtown. We kept it when we moved from here just in case. Well, it looks like a garage, and the front is, but there's a crash pad in the back."

Jeremy clapped Pax on the shoulder. "Let's load the vans and go."

"We need photos of the attackers for possible facial recognition." Garrett's flat voice stopped them all from scurrying away. He pinned Davis in his glare. "Bring the bodies to the motel so the cleaners can take them in one dump."

"Cleaners?" Sara's voice wobbled on the word.

The vision of what those people did was pretty clear in Meredith's mind. Her stomach heaved at the thought of bodies being loaded on stacks like cut firewood. "I'm guessing we don't want to know."

Jeremy put the keys in his back pocket. "Pax, you take Joel—"

Garrett's cold voice cut through the rustle of clothing

and halted footsteps. "He rides with me. I'll call Ellis and ask him to do some background."

Joel's eyes bulged. "On me?"

Garrett didn't hesitate. "Yes."

Suddenly Meredith felt less safe. It was one thing to battle strangers, but she knew from experience sometimes the people closest were the most dangerous.

STEPHEN NODDED TO the guard, then watched the door close behind him.

Bruce recognized the signs. Bloodshot eyes with shaking hands. Rather than worry about his lawyer's potential addictions, Bruce added this information to the list of ways to control Stephen.

This just proved his theory that people who claimed to be powerful often handed you the ammunition to destroy them. You just had to be patient. He was.

He was also smart enough not to be brought down by the drugs he peddled or women he purchased for a few nights of fun. Weakness had no place in his world. The weak died young, and he planned to stay on top for longer than any leader before him.

He sniffed. "Scotch, isn't it?"

Stephen stopped in the middle of sitting down. "What did you say?"

"You shouldn't drink your breakfast. One of these days your partners will find out, brand you a risk and cut you loose." Bruce liked the scenario so much he decided to make it happen the second he no longer needed the obese fool. "However, will young Conrad finish his studies without Daddy's money?"

Stephen ground his teeth together. "I am not going to keep running back and forth between my office and the prison every day."

"You are if I say you are." Bruce crossed one leg over the other and leaned back in his chair. "Now, what's the message?"

"Negative."

His lazy amusement vanished. Not the answer he expected or wanted. It took every ounce of restraint in his body not to flip over the table and curse Jeremy Hill. The man had shadowed him, wormed his way into the organization then cut him with his betrayal. Being played, realizing he'd let his enemy walk right into his house, ate away at Bruce's gut.

Hill would die but not from a well-aimed gunshot. No, he'd go out screaming in pain and begging for mercy, which would not come. The woman with him would go first and Jeremy would be forced to watch her skin be flayed and hear every scream.

Bruce balled his fists on his lap under the table and fought not to let Stephen see his rabid anger. "Anything else?"

The fat piece of garbage smiled. "He's not alone."

Bruce schooled his features. This was a setback but not the end. What Stephen didn't know, what no one, especially the Hill brothers knew, was that Bruce had an inside man. A guy tucked away and unrelated to Jeremy's work, who was prepared to take out the Hill brothers. The man sat in the prime position to hurt Jeremy through his weakness. Garrett.

"Interesting message," Bruce said as he rubbed his chin.

"Care to tell me what this all means?" Stephen waved his hand. "Forget it. Instead of plotting and doing whatever it is you're doing, we should work on your defense."

*Wrong answer.* "I need out of here today."

"The prosecutor will argue against bail." Stephen

shook his head as he talked. "With your open access to money, and due to the nature of the crime and your ties to Mexico—"

"All legitimate business contacts." In the drug trade, but he'd covered those tracks. He'd learned his lesson after showing Jeremy his tunnels, boasting about the easy access into the country by going under it, and then waking to Border Patrol officers at his front door.

Stephen cleared his throat. "You will be considered a flight risk. That's hard to get around."

"I'm not going anywhere. My business is here."

"Not having a family, no wife or children, is also a problem."

Only a lawyer would grab on to something so meaningless. "Since when does my marital status matter to the judicial system?"

"It all goes to show that you would have no problem picking up your life and leaving." Stephen took a small notebook and his shiny pen out of his inside jacket pocket and twisted the cap. "Other than business associates and employees, who else will be there in support of you today?"

"I'm a man devoted to work."

"You're proving my point." Stephen tapped the pen against the lined pages in an insipid jumpy beat. "What about that woman you were with when we talked a few months ago. Selina or Serena, whatever her name was."

"Serena and she's gone." *The disloyal bitch.*

"That's unfortunate."

"Certainly is poor timing. I'll give you that. But then, much about Serena turned out to be a nuisance."

She'd dropped Hill right in front of him and vouched for his credentials. Bruce had checked him out but the background had been faked. While he gained trust, she took photos, passed information.

No, her being gone was inevitable. The only mistake he made was in waiting so long to get rid of her. He was paying for that now.

Stephen scribbled a note. "Women are like that, but one would be useful here."

"In this case it was more useful for her to be gone."

"Are you sure there isn't something we could do to bring her back on a temporary basis?"

"Positive. She outwore her welcome."

Which was why she was dead. And she would soon have company as Hill watched another woman bleed out at his feet.

## Chapter Thirteen

Sara nibbled on her lip as she walked the line between the kitchenette counter and the folding table in front of it. Dawn had broken an hour ago and she hadn't slept in what felt like a year.

And she was stuck in a room with Meredith. The togetherness should have upset her. Meredith was part of Garrett's subterfuge, one for which she still didn't have a great explanation. If Sara were dealing with a guy other than Garrett, she probably would have written him off as a liar and a cheat and done something more violent than slapping him.

But he was Garrett. Secretive and imperfect and always dodging the hard questions, but her mind never jumped to the label of cheater. Maybe she was naive and stupid. Wouldn't be the first time someone called her that. Her father never found her particularly worthy.

She'd been written out of the will and banished from the family compound in Kansas as punishment for not doing something more spectacular with her life, like investment banking. He'd made the public announcement at a family gathering as a way to break her spirit, and only when years of threats had failed to get his desired response. But he'd actually freed her. She didn't have a problem with people making money, but she hated the theory that a person's bank account determined his or her value in society.

She glanced at Meredith. She sat at the small kitchen table and drummed her fingers on the top. Much faster and she'd hammer her way straight through the flimsy wood to the floor. "You want to be in that room."

Meredith looked up. "Don't you?"

"I'm not sure watching Garrett work would be good for our relationship." Sara slid into the chair across from the woman she'd been prepared to hate. No matter how hard she tried she couldn't summon up the requisite level of distrust or disgust.

She'd watched Meredith around Garrett and waited for a sign, any sign, that they shared something more than a lease. No stray looks or subtle touches. No, Meredith saved all those for Jeremy. Any idiot could see the woman had picked the brother she wanted and it wasn't Garrett.

"I'm happy to hear you still have one. With Garrett, I mean."

Sara wished she had the confidence in their ability to find their way through this. She could forgive a lot, but not alone. He had to change. Going back to playing the role of the mute, supportive fiancée didn't appeal to her. She feared her finding a backbone might be a deal breaker for him.

The idea of living without him had her swallowing to keep from gasping. "Yeah, well. We'll see."

She inhaled to stop the screaming in her head. She wanted to pound her fists and then pound on him for not seeing that she was the best thing to ever happen to him. When she finally wrestled her heart and her mind back under control, she heard only the gentle shushing sound of Meredith rubbing her hands together and the steady drip of the faucet.

"Nothing ever happened between us," she blurted out. "We really just were landlord and tenant."

Sara was surprised it had taken the woman this long to broach the subject. She didn't exactly seem like the bide-her-time type.

"So many lies," Sara whispered under her breath. When Meredith's eyes widened, Sara knew she had heard.

Meredith put her palms on the table and started to stand up. "We don't know each other, but I'm not lying. I don't know who—"

"Sit." Sara waved her off then poured them both another cup of coffee. "I know."

"You do?"

"I'm not an idiot. I can see you're attracted to Jeremy."

"That's nothing. It's just…" Meredith fell back into her seat with a clunk as the legs smacked against the floor.

"Yes?"

Meredith blew out a long breath. "Really? I have no idea what it is."

When Sara threw back her head and laughed, Meredith joined her. Like that, the winding tension snapped.

"I've known the guy for five seconds and it feels like forever."

"The Hill boys have that sort of effect on women. They're like a disease."

"If life were fair there would be a shot we could take to get over it or least build up immunity to them."

"If only."

Sara wrapped her fingers around the mug. Despite the summer heat, she'd been chilled since leaving the motel. In her head she knew it was some sort of reaction to the mayhem, but her body wouldn't listen. Even now her bones rattled hard enough to set her teeth chattering.

The amusement gave way to reality. "He never told me about the house in Coronado."

"That part is weird even for Mr. My Life Is Oh So Secret. No matter how I twist the facts, I can't make that part fit." Meredith shrugged. "I can't imagine how tough it is for you."

That was the problem. Sara worried that her reaction to the lie made her a doormat. The house didn't bother her as much as the pitying looks everyone was throwing her way suggested it should. Her fury came when she put all the facts together into one long, never-ending lie topped off with an I-need-my-space excuse.

She tried to explain what she still didn't understand in her own head. "It's typical of Garrett. He was keeping the different parts of his life separate."

"I still don't get it."

"I was over here in the apartment, the place he went when business was over." She slapped her hand down at one end of the table. "Once he proposed, he had our relationship all wrapped up and settled in his mind." She put her other hand at the opposite end. "His work was over here, along with the house and the motel and the warehouse downtown."

"And he inherited me when he bought the place. I always wondered why I didn't get kicked out when he moved in."

"A woman living alone and working as a teacher? Yeah, he would have had a soft spot for you. Can't imagine him making you leave." In the pros and cons list that made up Garrett, that one sat firmly in the pro column. He couldn't resist a person in need.

Meredith snorted. "I know you're blinded by love and all, but he's not exactly a soft guy."

"It's buried deep, but there." Sara knew that much.

Knew it down to her soul. "His mom was a teacher. She worked two jobs to put herself through college so she could eventually support them and see them every day in the school halls."

"Impressive lady."

"I doubt Garrett even realizes that in his head he was saving you." The reason seemed obvious to Sara, but that was because she watched and listened. She made him her priority and learned every scrap he dropped for her to find.

Maybe she really was pathetic.

"He never even told me he was the owner. I started sending my rent check to a corporation with a post office box address."

"I'm sure it made sense in his head. I've spent most of our relationship being baffled by the things he shares and the things he chooses to hide." And the surprises chipped away at her but were livable…until the one where he walked out.

Meredith took a long drink. "Men are idiots."

"Some, yeah. Even those who generally aren't seem to dabble in idiocy from time to time."

Meredith eyed Sara over the rim of her mug. "You still love him."

She didn't bother to deny it. Loving Garrett had never been the issue. Never would be the problem. "So, what does that make me?"

"Human."

If Sara hadn't liked Meredith before that moment, she would have started right then.

The bond was tenuous, but she decided to share anyway. "We broke up because he wanted to elope."

"Since I'm not seeing his idiocy in that piece, I'm thinking there's more to this story."

"Less, actually. He was looking for a quickie marriage with no friends or family present. No flowers or dress. He didn't even see the point of buying rings."

"Now I'm getting it." Meredith shook her head. "Dear, deluded Garrett."

"That was his pitch. Just us and a sterile room with some random guy in a suit officiating. It would take a few minutes—he actually said that as if it were a selling point—and then we'd go back home so he could ship out on his next assignment and I could go back to work."

Meredith whistled. "The wedding no little girl has ever dreamed of."

"Exactly."

The memory of his pitch still left Sara reeling. She'd chuckled while he laid it all out, thinking it had to be a bad joke. But no.

"And you sell wedding dresses for a living, right? Did he not take that as a hint?"

Funny how Meredith got it, but after almost two years together Garrett didn't. "I'm the assistant manager. I hope to own the shop one day."

Meredith rolled her eyes. "Like I said, idiots."

"Yep."

They fell into a comfortable silence. The low rumble of male voices seeped through the wall beside them.

Sara tapped her fingernail against the ceramic mug. When she couldn't stand it anymore, she piped up. "So, back to you and Jeremy…"

Meredith shook her head hard enough to lose her balance and have to adjust her feet where they were tucked under her. "It's a heat-of-the-moment thing."

"Interesting."

"Nothing serious or even worth talking about."

"Uh-huh."

"You sound like you don't believe me."

*Not one bit.* "Do *you* believe the nonsense you're spouting?"

"Hey, what happened to the quiet woman in the corner?"

"She almost died in a fireball." The near-death thing had Sara thinking she needed to yell more. "I have eyes, Meredith. He looks at you like he wants to throw his body over yours and you look like you'd happily let him."

"That about sums it up."

"At least it's mutual." Sara tried to sell the point Meredith seemed comfortable with, but figured she'd failed when Meredith shot her a you've-got-to-be-kidding expression.

"It's so complicated." The tabletop tapping started again. She lowered her head as if she wanted to bang that against the wood, as well.

Sara stopped any chance of that by putting her hand over Meredith's. "It doesn't have to be."

"You're saying that, with the state of your relationship with Garrett?"

That little truth stung. She rubbed her chest to make it go away. "Call me an optimist."

"I shouldn't have—"

"Ask me whatever you want to ask me."

It took another minute of shifting in her chair before Meredith got the words out. "Is Jeremy like Garrett? If I go deeper, do I get to relive all the garbage you've been through? Because I don't think it will work. You are much more patient that I am."

"You mean gullible and pathetic." Sara fell back in her chair.

"I really didn't." Meredith stared at Sara as if willing her to believe.

"Thank you for that. Sometimes I feel like I am, so it's nice to hear it might not be true." And she meant it because, for whatever reason, Meredith's image of her did matter.

"But the question still stands."

Since Sara knew the question was coming, she didn't hesitate now that it had arrived. "Yes, but more grounded. They both seek danger and fall into those rescuing patterns. There's something lighter about Jeremy."

"I think I missed that part of him."

"Oh, don't get me wrong. He can brood, but the darkness doesn't swallow him. Not like it does with Garrett. He watched men he worked with and cared about die in a truck bomb during the war in Iraq. He carries the horror of those deaths with him always. He views the moment as his failure, not that even he could have stopped it."

"That's a pretty big piece of baggage."

"Loving them isn't easy." Sara stared at Meredith's tapping hands.

Meredith followed her gaze and flattened her palms against the tabletop. "That's not relevant since I've known him less than two days."

"Oh, you're missing my point. Falling for the Hill men is easy."

"Tell me about it," she grumbled.

"It's the sticking around part that will kill you." Sara thought about the last twenty-four hours. "Possibly really kill you."

"That's not very reassuring."

She had to smile at that. "I was going for honest."

Meredith leaned back in her chair and continued to click her fingernails. "You know, I like you. You're stronger than you look. Tougher."

"I've learned the hard way to stand up for what I want." And had paid a huge price so far.

After two sharp knocks, the door opened and Jeremy stuck his head in. "May I come in?"

Sara hid her smile as she got up and dumped her mug in the sink. "I was leaving anyway."

"You going to harness yourself to the roof?" Meredith asked with more than a little amusement in her voice.

"Something a bit more simple, like go into the bathroom."

Meredith's eyebrow lifted. "You don't have to run on our account."

"Maybe I'll take a bath while I'm in there."

Poor Jeremy stood there looking all masculine and confused. "Uh, you'll have to do it in the sink because there's no tub."

Sara winked at him as she left the room. "You guys sure do know how to show women a good time."

"You two seem to be getting along okay." Jeremy stood just inside the door with his arms stiff at his sides.

"Are you surprised?"

"A little, but also relieved. I'm pretty fond of Sara in a she's-perfect-for-my-brother sort of way."

"I didn't think so at first, but that was me being all judgy and dumb." Meredith shook her head at the embarrassing memory.

"Excuse me?"

"I mistook her love for Garrett as weakness. Now I get it. There's no pretense. She's not looking to battle the world. She's solid and Garrett definitely needs solid because, frankly, he's a bit out of control, especially over this Joel thing."

"That must have been some conversation with Sara."

"We muddled through and figured each other out."

"I'm always stunned by the resilience of women." Jeremy glanced at the closed bathroom door. "I'm not as sure at this moment about the men I know."

Dark circles streaked under his eyes as if exhaustion dragged at him. His shirt had come untucked and his hair fell over his forehead, giving him a less severe look than his brother. But despair shimmered all around him.

Meredith wanted to rush over and rain kisses on his face until he smiled again. But that was crazy. He was in the middle of a tense situation. And then there was the part where they barely knew each other.

She stayed in her seat. "Did you think you'd come in and find us pulling each other's hair and rolling across the floor?"

A smile tugged at the corner of his mouth as he stared at the floor. "Sort of. Stupid male fantasy, I guess."

"The women wrestling thing? Figures." He wiggled his eyebrows, so she dropped the subject. "Once she figured out I wasn't making a play for Garrett, we were fine."

Jeremy's blue eyes sparked with life. "Is there anyone you are thinking about making a play for?"

"Subtle."

"I wasn't trying to be." He walked over to her. Stalked, really.

Long and lean, he closed the gap in only two steps. Her head fell back to look up at him. With his palms on the arms of her chair, he blocked her in until his warmth surrounded her.

He crouched down until they were eye-to-eye. His broad shoulders blocked out the room behind her. Everything else fell away. Faded into nothing, until it was only the two of them.

This close, the butterflies in her stomach flapped

harder. Her heartbeat hadn't danced a jig for a man in a long time. It scared her that it danced for this one.

"How are things going in there?" she asked, trying to keep her balance while everything around her spun.

"Not great." He dropped to his knees with his face just inches from hers.

He tried to hide the wince but she caught it.

Guilt washed over her. She'd forgotten all about his injury. Bandages and over-the-counter meds couldn't replace good hospital care. But he was so stubborn.

"Your side." She touched her hand to the space right above the bandage. "Are you okay?"

"I'm better now that I'm right here."

"Jeremy." Her thumb slipped over the bandage bringing relief when he didn't double over. "That's sweet, but I doubt it's medically accurate to say seeing someone cures pain."

"I wanted to get out of there."

She felt the words against her mouth. Her mind struggled to stay on topic when his hands moved down to her hips and pulled her forward. "Away from Garrett's fury and Joel's denials?"

"To be with you." He traced her chin with a line of small kisses.

"Oh."

"That's it?" His mouth found the sensitive patch of skin behind her ear.

She shivered, trembling as his lips traveled down to the side of her neck and stayed there. Hot and wet, the gentle sucking stole her breath and had her head falling farther toward her shoulder.

"I'm not sure what to say." She was stunned she could form any words at all.

"Then how about letting me take the lead?"

Before she could answer, his mouth closed over hers. The sweet memory of their first kiss vanished under the intensity of the second. Firm lips gave way to the sweep of his tongue. Her hands fell to his shoulders. Her body lifted off the chair as he pulled her to the front and against his chest.

Slanting as she breathed him in. Caressing his mouth with hers. The kiss shut off her mind and opened up a door inside her she'd slammed shut years ago. With the touch of his mouth her world to her abandoned dreams and hopes reopened.

It was a kiss of longing and promise. She didn't know she craved it until she had it.

He pulled back and rested his forehead against hers. "I needed that."

He sounded as breathless as she felt. "Happy I was here to help."

He lifted his head, letting his gaze brush over her face as his fingertips outlined her lips. "You're the *only* one I needed."

"Jeremy."

Turning his head, he kissed the soft inside of her arm. "When this is over…"

He led a violent life. Walked in and out of danger. Led with a gun and didn't hesitate to put his body in the line of fire.

When this was over they would be, too.

But part of her wanted to believe. "Yes?"

"We'll figure it out then." With one last kiss on her forehead, he got up and went back into the garage.

A long time later her heart returned to its regular

steady beat. But not before it swelled and thumped and reminded her what it felt like to care for a man.

Turned out Sara was right. Falling for a Hill brother was far too easy.

## Chapter Fourteen

Bruce lounged on his bunk with his arm folded under his head. In the other hand he twirled the piece of wadded-up paper the guard had dropped between the bars of his cell on his regular walk down the corridor.

He'd been to the courthouse and back first thing that morning. No bail. The white-haired bitch of a judge with the fake nails and caked-on lipstick called him a flight risk. She talked about previous allegations and the severity of the charges against him.

She had no idea what a danger he could be.

The judge's finding served as another setback but not a death knell. She'd left the door open for bail review. More importantly, he got out in the fresh air for more than an hour. Breaking free felt good, but passing a note to the guard who escorted him up the elevator from the small court jail had been the real goal. Bruce knew the courier had been successful because his fingers wrapped around the paper that held his answer.

Pass some cash. Make a promise. Have a guy on the outside collect on a debt or deliver a message with his fists to someone who needed the pressure before he could perform. Gathering intel came easy when you knew what people needed and how to get it for them. Gaining loyalty took time, but being a man others could depend on for payment sped the process.

And the supposed upstanding members of society were even easier to handle than the criminal element. Dig for a nasty secret held by someone in an official capacity—those little bits of information they didn't want anyone to know. Feed the habit, no matter what it was, then take a few photos and deliver them at the right time.

Bruce's favorite trick involved sending a messenger to the house while the wife was home. Amazing how a man snapped into line when he hovered on the brink of having his depravity unmasked on his own turf.

And it sure paid to have sources everywhere. Bruce's prearranged signals consisted of a few words and came as each step in the plan hatched. Stephen could sneak in the important information relative to those points.

But that wasn't why Bruce used Stephen. Bruce did it to exert control. To remind Stephen he was on the payroll. It was a way of keeping him in line.

The guards picked up the rest of the slack. Even now Bruce twirled the paper ball through his fingers. After torturing himself with the waiting, he took his reward.

Sitting up, he unwrapped the paper from his guy inside Hill's team and stared at the message typed there.

*Close proximity. Will proceed.*

There was only one answer: move in and destroy him. Bruce smiled at the thought.

Oh, how he wished he could be there to watch Jeremy Hill, the man Bruce once knew by another name and trusted with the intricate details of his operation, bleed out in a dirty alley on a forgotten street somewhere. Bruce hoped it would take long, hot days to find him. Jeremy deserved a slow, terrifying death.

Closing his eyes, Bruce inhaled, blocking out the

smell of stale air and urine that filled every inch of the filthy prison, and imagined an endless supply of free air. Soon Jeremy would be dead. Burned, beaten, shot, and if there was any justice, broken after seeing his woman and brother ripped to pieces.

All Bruce had to do now was wait for the confirmation of the end. Then he'd give the okay for Stephen to try another bail hearing. After that, Bruce would never enter a cell again.

Knowing it was about to happen had to be enough.

The revenge would be so sweet.

JEREMY STOOD BEHIND Joel's chair, leaning against a small table. With his injured side, he couldn't hold his body up without help. They'd set the chair in the dead center of the vacant garage. Davis said they hadn't had cars there in over a year, but the smell of gasoline permeated the walls and fell around them.

There wasn't a big spotlight shining on Joel or handcuffs locking him to the chair. They'd abandoned the dramatics because they'd all had enough for one day. Possibly for a lifetime.

From the way Davis and Pax kept to the side, the goal was clear. They were all going to sit there until they were satisfied Joel was clean...or not.

They'd been at it for an hour already. Swearing and grumbling, Joel had handed over his phone and weapons for standard checks. He'd answered questions and his story never changed.

After the hours of constant exertion, they were all tired. No one had the heart for this, even though it had to be done. So, when Garrett started in for another round, Pax shook his head and began walking around the edge of the garage.

Jeremy glanced over at his brother where he sat in a chair across from Joel. Jeremy knew the situation was eating away at Garrett. He gave his team all the tools to get the jobs done and never hid behind a desk. He'd only send his men out if he went along. If they ran into danger, so would he. They were all in it together. Always.

He required loyalty in return. Having someone so close to him, someone he hand-selected, betray him would cause weeks, maybe months, of reassessing what he'd missed. It would eat Garrett alive.

Especially if the culprit was Joel. Like all new hires, he'd gotten through the questions and drug tests and background check. He took his polygraph, but that part always came after the job started.

Jeremy knew Garrett had taken the extra step and fought to rush through Joel's DIA security clearance. That made the potential blow even bigger. Ego mixed with an emotional upheaval. They were wrapped up in this to the point they couldn't be separated again.

Garrett's chair scraped against the cement floor as he leaned forward with his elbows balanced on his knees. His mouth opened then closed again. "I hate this."

Instead of his usual cool detachment, Garrett met this challenge with defeat showing in his eyes. Jeremy stepped up. "Our attackers like fire. Is that your specialty?"

Joel flopped back. "I can't believe this."

"Me either," Pax said while Davis mumbled in agreement.

"You two can leave if you can't take it," Garrett yelled over his shoulder.

"No way," Davis and Pax said at the same time.

Garrett didn't let up. "Tell me why I'm wrong."

"How am I supposed to prove a negative?"

Joel had a decent point. They were asking him to do

the impossible—convince them he didn't do anything he wasn't supposed to do. They didn't have any evidence of wrongdoing. Just a set of odd coincidences. It was a shame neither he nor Garrett believed in those.

"You're the newest guy. Maybe you thought you could earn some money on the side, get in with Darren." If so, he wouldn't be the first guy to double-dip. The first on Garrett's team, yeah, but it wouldn't be the first time a federal agent collected an extra paycheck on the side.

Joel crossed his arms over his stomach and his legs at his heels. "I'm not selling information."

"Are we sure this is about Darren?" Davis asked.

Garrett continued to stare down at his hands. "Who else could be at the bottom of this?"

Davis moved back into the tight circle. "How about any one of the hundred people Jeremy has taken down? We have a list of enemies. It could be any one of hundreds of people."

Garrett finally lifted his head. "This isn't an attack on the team. It's on me. My house. My people. I'm the one who set Darren up."

"With my help." Joel sat up straight, staring at Garrett with renewed intensity. "So, why would I have done that only to double-cross you now?"

"Deep cover."

Joel shook his head. "You've lost your mind. Both of you. Whatever is in your gene pool is messed up."

Not the first time Jeremy had heard that. He'd actually thought the same thing once or twice. "Let's run through the night at the motel one more time."

Garrett's phone rang and he opened it before the second ring. They all sat in silence, including Garrett. He never said a word until he hung up. "We have company."

"More attackers?" Davis's voice carried a faraway

quality of disbelief. "This proves it can't be Joel. He's been right here, with all of us watching the whole time."

"This visitor doesn't carry a gun. At least I don't think he does." Garrett stood up. "Ellis is here."

The information didn't make any sense. Jeremy tried to figure out what it meant. "Your boss?"

"Why is he in town?" Pax asked.

"Let's find out." Garrett nodded toward the door, pointing to Davis. "Go get him. He'll likely have his Secret Service detail with him, but double-check any guy who comes in with him."

"Wait, you mean he's actually here? In San Diego instead of D.C.?" Joel asked. His eyes were as wide as the rest of the team's.

"Gentlemen." Ellis walked in, his expensive shoes tapping against the hard floor. A younger man raced behind him with his arms loaded down while Ellis carried nothing.

Jeremy had met the department head before, during an awards ceremony for Garrett after a particularly difficult case. Ellis looked more like a political appointee than a career bureaucrat who spent his day sitting behind a desk. He wore a perfectly tailored gray suit and everything from his tie to his hair stayed in place as he moved.

And the man could work a room. He'd already shaken the hand of every team member, including Joel, and worked his way back around to Jeremy.

Ellis held out his hand. "Good to see you again."

"Thank you, sir."

"This is Andrew." Before anyone could even glance in the young man's direction or ask his last name, Ellis started talking again. "I hear we have a problem."

"More than one," Jeremy pointed out.

Garrett didn't try to hide his frustration. "Why are you here?"

Not the most politically smart question, but an honest one. Ellis didn't appear to mind. He took in Garrett's mood and the pulsing anger in the room and ignored it all.

"Fires, explosions, missing agents. I figured I had better come out here and see what was happening." Ellis reached a hand out and Andrew shoved a file in it.

After all the doubts and pacing, Pax stepped up. "We think Darren is going after Garrett."

Ellis nodded in Joel's direction. "And this is about what? Doesn't exactly look like a team meeting and from the urgent request for background information, I assume this is deeper than Aunt Susie having financial trouble and threatening his clearance."

To his credit, Garrett didn't let anyone speak for him this time. He shifted until he stood directly in front of his boss. "There was some suspicious behavior, and since we seem to have a mole, we investigated."

"Suspicious?"

"Nothing we need to discuss."

"I see." Ellis shut the file with a clap. "You picked Joel for your team. Convinced me he was right for these assignments without more hours in the field on less dangerous assignments."

Joel's eyes widened as if he were hearing the information for the very first time.

Garrett ignored the stunned silence. "And I still believe in him."

Ellis's eyebrow lifted. "Really?"

"I had no choice but to put him through the gauntlet and I think he knows that."

Joel nodded, even though the doubt was clear on every line of his face. "Yes."

"Find anything interesting? Do I need to contact our security experts for an assessment?" Ellis paged through his file as he talked.

"No." Jeremy suspected his brother's one-word answer satisfied Ellis. Jeremy also got the distinct impression Ellis wasn't reading. That this whole production was for show and that whatever he intended to say would hit like a bomb.

"Well, I have more bad news." He closed the file and put it under his arm. "This, all the firepower and destruction, is not coming from Darren."

Garrett's mouth dropped open. "It has to be."

They all shuffled their feet as they got the news they dreaded to hear. To Jeremy, the confirmation shattered the fragile sense of confidence brewing inside him.

Knowing the enemy made fighting him possible. Hard but doable. But some random attacker with a grudge among many took fighting to a new and dangerous level.

Garrett could die. Meredith and Sara were in the crosshairs, as well. The sudden pounding in Jeremy's head wiped out the pain in his side.

"I ran everything on him. Have checked every angle and had him watched every second. It's someone else." Ellis drilled Joel with a scowl. "You know anything about that?"

"No, sir."

Andrew stayed behind Ellis, moving as he moved, juggling files and a phone and what looked like a travel coffee cup. He'd put the laptop on the floor. One more turn and he'd trip over the thing and be on top of Jeremy.

He saw it coming and started to issue a warning when Andrew kicked the computer over and careened right into him. Jeremy held out a hand to steady the younger man, but the crash happened anyway.

The phone bounced against the hard ground. Coffee sloshed over the cup and folders scattered across the floor in a swoosh.

"Sorry," Andrew mumbled as he moved away.

Jeremy didn't make a big deal of the bumbling because Ellis's frown said enough. He didn't move until his assistant picked up everything and stood up straight again.

"Are you done?" he said, his voice dripping with disdain.

"Sorry, sir," Andrew mumbled without looking up.

Ellis waited one more second then addressed the team. "I think we need to regroup and rethink suspects."

From the space of one sentence to another, Jeremy made a firm decision. "I'll be out, but available by phone for a few hours."

Ellis's expression turned deadly cold. "You have somewhere better to be?"

Jeremy ignored him and looked at Garrett. "I need to get Meredith out of here. As soon as I know she's set up and safe, I'll be back. Sara?"

Garrett shook his head. "She stays with me."

Jeremy wished he could say the same thing, have the same conviction about Meredith. Leaving her in a safe spot was the right thing, but it would kill him. The idea of her being hurt because of him, because of knowing his family, pushed bile up his throat. He'd battled through fear and danger his entire life, but this threatened to freeze him.

He didn't even know where to hide her. He lived like a nomad and his one decent place had been torched. That limited his options, especially since the place would have to be secure. Not many of those around. He didn't want a traditional safe house because as far as he could tell they weren't all that safe.

Any place seemed like a risk, but Garrett needed him, too. Jeremy couldn't tolerate the thought of letting either of them down, so he would leave and come back, even if it meant walking back into fire.

Loyalties battled inside him. His body ached and his brain screamed for him to take Meredith to bed and not crawl out again for a week.

"You need to stay." Ellis waved his hand in the air as if saying the words made them so. "Andrew can take care of Ms. Samms."

Not a surprise Ellis knew Meredith's name. He likely knew a lot more. She'd hate that. It felt like an invasion of privacy even though it was standard policy. She'd lived in Garrett's house. That meant Ellis would have a file on her just like he did on every one of them.

Despite all Ellis's power and the certain way he spoke, Jeremy's answer was the same. All that power, Ellis practically glowed from it, and Jeremy had to defy it.

"No, I won't be staying."

"Jeremy." Garrett said his name as a warning.

Understandable but Jeremy had to go with his gut on this one. The attacks kept coming. Meredith refused to stay out of sight. So long as she was determined to pick up a gun, he was equally set on keeping her safe.

For now that meant getting her out of there. When Davis nodded and Garrett didn't put up much of a verbal fight, Jeremy knew his instincts were right on this one.

Ellis, however, was not convinced. He was a man accustomed to having his orders followed, and balked when the acquiescence wasn't automatic.

His eyes narrowed as he ran a finger over his mustache. "I'm not sure you heard me."

*Heard and ignored.* "With all due respect, I don't work for you."

"That's a good thing since I don't tolerate insubordination. People who work for me listen and obey, or they don't work for me for very long."

"Which is probably why it's good I picked Border Patrol." Jeremy matched Ellis's battle stance with one of his own. "And I'm on mandatory leave from that job at the moment."

"Ah, yes. The injury."

Just the mention of it made the skin around it itch and the scar thump in pain. "It's healing."

Garrett stepped up. "Sir, if I may—"

"No." After a moment of silence, a smile broke across Ellis's face. "It would appear the family resemblance goes deeper than looks. Your stubborn streak certainly feels familiar."

Jeremy nodded. "We are twins."

"One of you is enough for DIA. I'm not sure the agency could handle both."

A wave of relief swept the room. The tension choking the room snapped with the amusement in Ellis's voice.

Jeremy felt his shoulders fall. He didn't even know he was holding his body stiff until the wind rushed out of him.

Pax slipped his keys out of his pocket and caught everyone's attention with the jingling. "Davis and I will drive."

"Thanks, but no. You're needed here." Jeremy didn't want to take the crowd with him. The goal was to remove Meredith from the danger, not drag it along behind them.

"Someone could be waiting outside and you need to throw them off your trail," Pax said, and Davis nodded in agreement.

"What are you suggesting?" Garrett asked.

"Pax and I drive the cars. Meredith and Jeremy will

be in the back of one. When it's clear, Jeremy will get in the driver's seat and go wherever he's going. Pax and I will come home."

"My detail came in matching black SUVs. You are free to use them so long as you bring them both back." Ellis snapped his fingers at Andrew. "We need to talk to the detail."

Andrew frowned. "Your guards won't agree."

"They don't get a say."

Not about to refuse help, Jeremy jumped to agree. "I'll be out of here within the next fifteen minutes."

Ellis shot him a level stare. "Where are you going?"

If there was a mole, Jeremy wasn't taking a chance. "I'll know when I get there."

## Chapter Fifteen

Ducked down on the floor of an SUV, balancing on the balls of her feet with a loaded weapon sitting just inches from her face, Meredith marveled at what her life had become. She battled little kids on a weekly basis. Tried to get them to quiet down, take their fingers out of their noses and stop slapping each other. Most days her biggest challenge consisted of a stray peanut and an allergy emergency.

Hiding with Jeremy as they raced along the roads southeast of San Diego in a vehicle driven by a man she barely knew was well out of her comfort zone. Then again, so was Jeremy. The accountant who took her to dinner two weeks ago couldn't carry a conversation let alone a gun. A little boredom sounded good right about now.

Jeremy tapped his finger on her arm. "You okay?"

She glanced up into serious eyes that didn't quite go with the amused voice. The determination was there, but so was concern.

*Yeah, forget the accountant.*

She decided to go with humor as a way of taking some of Jeremy's tension away. "Your second date choice isn't much better than the first. You should think about dinner and a movie. Heck, fast food and a DVD would be a huge improvement."

"Next time we'll do anything you want."

Her heart hiccuped. "Will there be a next time?"

"I'll make sure there is." His fingers circled her wrist, light and so smooth that her pulse jumped at his touch.

"You do that."

"You guys know I'm here, right?" Pax looked up. When his gaze went past them in the backseat, his smile disappeared and he jerked the wheel hard to the right.

Her equilibrium abandoned her as he skidded around a corner and she fell on her butt for the second time. The tires squealed and her head bounced off the door handle. "Ouch."

She rubbed the newest bruise and was grateful she'd stopped counting them. She'd acquired more in the last two days than she had in the previous twelve years.

The only thing keeping her from whining was the knowledge of the huge gash in Jeremy's side. Every time he replaced a bandage, he removed a red scrap of material that had started out white. Much more of this and he'd have a raging infection. It might only slow him down for two seconds, but the idea of him in more pain touched off a buzzing in her ears.

"That was rough." He put his gun on the seat and helped her back up. "I'm thinking you're missing your center of gravity."

"It sure seems that way." She did seem to bounce around much more than he did. Score one for being bigger. Sara was so tiny she'd probably sail through a window.

"Pax?" Jeremy knocked his fist against the back of the driver's seat in front of him. "You want to slow down before we throw up back here?"

"Can't."

Jeremy's head tilted to the side. "Why?"

"I think we have a tail." Tension vibrated in Pax's voice and in the way he kept clenching and unclenching the steering wheel.

"Of course we do. Makes sense in light of the last few days." She didn't even bother to panic. Her insides were jumping long before Pax's verification. On some level she knew danger would follow them even if they drove to Denver. If her theory was right, being next to Jeremy just might be the most dangerous place in the world.

He tapped his finger against the transmitter in his ear. "Davis, any tail?"

Without an earpiece, she had no idea what the answer was. She tugged on Jeremy's sleeve to get his attention. "What did he say?"

Pax answered her. "Nothing on his end."

"Looks like it's just us." Jeremy blew out a long breath as he spoke.

"Interesting."

Jeremy went to work checking his weapons. "You're taking this well."

With her elbow on the seat, Meredith leaned down and rubbed the growing bump on the back of her head. "Only on the outside."

Jeremy froze. Only his eyes moved as his gaze switched to her. "I'm sorry. I dragged you into all of this, me and Garrett. You never had a choice."

"You think I would have chosen no?"

"I wouldn't blame you if you did."

The woman she was before she met Jeremy would have said "no." She would have stayed in her house and played it safe because strong men meant dangerous men. Not now.

Knowing him even for a short time filled her with a strength she wished she'd had years ago. It was one thing to practice self-defense in the relative safety of a big room lined with mats. It was a totally different thing to fight off a real attack. She knew she could. She wouldn't freeze. She'd fight back. Knowing she had that power was a true gift.

"Just get us out of the mess."

Jeremy tapped on the back of Pax's seat again. "You heard the woman."

He shot her a smile through the rearview mirror. "Yes, ma'am."

The car took a sharp right turn. Meredith went flying to the left, directly toward Jeremy's shoulder. She curled her arms over her head and readied for the blow. Strong arms closed around her before she hit, but her weight sped up the momentum until they slammed against the door.

She squealed.

He groaned.

"We're going to be okay," he whispered in her ear.

Now she understood why all the textbooks told teachers to praise kids. Something about even a potentially empty boast restored her self-confidence. "I know."

She pushed away and balanced on her feet again, this time grabbing on to the passenger seat with both hands to keep steady. She knew Jeremy needed his hands free and his thoughts clear. Hanging all over him wasn't going to get either of those things done.

Jeremy poked his head between the front seats and leaned on the storage bin. He kept his body down as he talked to Pax. "What do you see?"

"A sedan behind us. No plates but looks like a newer model. Pretty expensive car." Pax rattled off the list in pure military style.

"How's his driving?"

"Erratic. He seems a step behind, but I turn suddenly then he turns. He's done this before."

"But he's not even trying to pretend he's not following." Jeremy made a statement instead of asking a question.

"No."

For some reason that news, the whole conversation, sent a new fissure of anxiety spinning through her. If the guy wasn't trying to hide his face or his purpose, he likely didn't think they would survive to identify him or his car. Worse, there might also be a second car somewhere.

The second after she thought it her body started shaking. She wedged her back against the door to keep Jeremy from seeing her new flash of fear. He had enough to worry about without trying to calm her down, as if that was even possible.

Jeremy picked that moment to swear. He lifted his chin as if trying to look over the backseat. "Can you make out a face?"

Pax gave a sharp shake of his head. "No. Tinted windows."

"How convenient," Jeremy mumbled.

Without thinking, Meredith blurted out the questions that kept playing in her mind. "How would anyone have known about the garage? It was Pax and Davis's secret, not Garrett's. I mean, would an enemy of Garrett's go looking for property his team owns?"

Jeremy's jaw clenched. "I was wondering the same thing."

"Common sense tells me that to find us at the garage someone would have to be watching and that means…" She let the thought trail off because saying it out loud would take her mind to a place she didn't want to go.

They'd had enough accusations and doubts swirling around them.

Jeremy grabbed on to the seats in front of him with a white-knuckle grip. "Inside information."

Her stomach did a nosedive to her feet. "So, Joel is crooked?"

Pax's gaze met hers in the mirror again. "No."

The car swerved and Jeremy fell back on her, pinning her against the seat. "Watch it."

She bit her bottom lip to keep from screaming, but having a hundred-and-ninety pounds balanced on her ankle brought tears to her eyes. "Uh, Jeremy? Could you shift?"

If he heard her, he didn't show it.

"Forget this." Pulling his body through the space between the seats, Jeremy crawled over the console. Not an easy feat for his wide shoulders.

When she blinked again, he'd jumped into the passenger seat next to Pax. She tried to grab him but ended up pulling his shirt out of his pants. "What are you doing? Someone will see you."

"No need to hide. He knows we're in here." Jeremy glared at her as he clicked the seat belt. "But you stay down. We don't need to hand the guy a target."

Jeremy balanced his palms against the dashboard. "Meredith, use your feet to brace your body."

"Why?"

"We're about to crash."

"What?" She screamed the question.

"Pax, turn into him," Jeremy shouted as the sedan crossed the double line and barreled up beside them.

A deep canyon yawned off to their right. Sharp brush and brown shrubs spread out for miles. One spin in there would trap them on a slope, and that was only if they survived the initial fall. Add in the dry trees and engine sparks, and disaster loomed all around them.

The sedan edged closer then swerved into the SUV. The force of the hit knocked Pax's hands off the wheel and pulled Jeremy's seat belt tight into his midsection, strangling him. He reached over to push the button and release the restraint, but it jammed.

"Hold on!" Pax shouted as he locked his arms.

Jeremy was about to warn him about tensing up when the car slammed into them a second time. The crack of metal against metal made the SUV shudder and slide. His mind went to Meredith in the back, bouncing around, not tied down.

Before he could reach out to her, his body shot back deep into the seat. He sprang back and his chest caved in as if something smashed into him with the force of a racing train. He heard his gun fall and tried to catch it, but everything happened too fast.

Jeremy tried to keep his eyes open and his body soft but the smash vibrated through every cell and jarred his back teeth. While his head lolled to the side, metal crunched against metal again. The smell of hot car and even hotter pavement wound around them. He opened his mouth to shout for her and realized the airbags had deployed.

The next hit bounced off the bumper. Smoke curled up from under the hood and metal crumpled in around them. Jeremy tried to calculate the risk of the gas tank exploding when the SUV went into a spin.

The world raced around them in a green-and-brown blur. His head rocked in time with the car until the merry-go-round made him dizzy. Round and round until he lost count and had to concentrate on not throwing up.

Tires screeched and the smell of burned rubber seeped

in through every window. Meredith's screams continued even after the car finally bounced to a halt, tipping and rocking. Through it all, the thread of panic in her high-pitched voice rattled in his brain.

He raised his hips, shimmied the knife out of his pocket and cut through the airbag until it lay deflated on his lap. Pax coughed and Jeremy saw long black skid marks on the road through the diagonal crack down the windshield.

They'd come to a halt perpendicular to the lane. If a car came in either direction, they'd be toast. Figured they'd land on a blind curve.

"Pax." Meredith's shaky hand reached through the seats to pull on Pax's arm. "Move."

Jeremy took in her frantic eyes and disheveled clothes. "Honey?"

But she wasn't looking at him. His gaze followed hers to the front of the car. His vision cleared just in time to see the sedan head right for them. The guy gunned it until the grills hit and one wheel of the SUV went over the cliff.

And it kept pushing. Slowly, as if to draw out every excruciating second, he inched them closer to oblivion and let them dangle there.

"Do something," Meredith pleaded as she rattled the door handles.

The wheels crunched on the gravel beneath them as the earth below them gave way. Pax hit the gas but the SUV's tires just spun. Jeremy didn't wait for a miracle or for his head to clear.

He would not die this way.

His shoulder throbbed and he could feel a warm trail of blood run down his stomach from his reopened wound. Scrambling, his hands in motion and fingers fumbling, he felt below his seat, patting as his heart thudded up to his ears.

He snatched the end of the gun just as the SUV started to slide farther into the canyon. Lifting his gun, he fired a shot straight through the driver's-side window.

The car pulled back, idling while the driver watched.

"Aim to the side. He's ducking."

Jeremy obeyed Pax's command and fired again. On the third, a body slumped over the wheel and the car began to roll with its wheels angled to the right and kept going until the front end crumpled against the rock wall on the inside of the lanes.

The SUV didn't stop either, it teetered on the edge of the cliff with its tires spinning and the engine revving with useless energy.

Pax moved the wheel and stomped on the brakes. "I can't stop it."

"Out."

Meredith rattled the handles and smacked the heel of her hand against the door. "I'm trapped."

"No. Not like this." Using every last ounce of strength inside him, Jeremy shoved and pushed and finally got his door open.

He reached behind him for Meredith's arm. This was going to hurt like hell. For both of them. The SUV rolled slowly at first, but it was picking up speed. In a minute or two it could flip over and they'd be dead.

Yanking her by the forearms, he pulled her through the opening between the seats. She hit the front seat and landed on his lap. He folded his body around her and leaned out the door, prepared for a diving roll.

She grabbed for the dashboard and stopped their momentum. "Wait."

"We have to go now." Over his anger and the raging pain in his side, he saw her reaching for Pax. "What are you—"

Seeing Pax's head fall to the side with his eyes closed and his body unmoving stopped Jeremy's big escape. "Give me your knife."

She dug around her pocket and slipped it out. With an arcing slice, he cut through Pax's seat belt. The car hit something hard and they all bounced, heads hitting against the ceiling right before the door popped opened.

Then Jeremy and Meredith went airborne. He fell backward, taking her with him. They tumbled for a few feet, half in the air, rocks cutting into their skin. Jeremy's head knocked against the hard ground as his back crashed into a set of bushes.

He pulled her out of the way just as the SUV raced by them. The wheels bounced against the packed dirt as the metal crunched and rumbled. When it hit an outcropping of rocks, the SUV tipped over.

They lay there not moving for a second. He touched a hand to her head. "You okay?"

"Yes." The voice sounded breathless and in more than a little awe.

"We have to—"

She raised her head. "Pax?"

The burst of energy had Jeremy sitting up. He patted his ankle for his spare gun and said a prayer of thanks when he found it still there. "Meredith, wait."

She moaned as she struggled to her feet. Her sneakers slipping, she hiked up with her left arm tucked against her stomach.

It took longer for Jeremy's head to clear. He'd made sure to take the brunt of the fall, but he could see streaks of blood on the back of her arm. He'd just finished his visual inventory of her injuries when he saw the lump on the ground in front of her.

She reached Pax's body where he lay on his stomach

in the dirt. Dropping to her knees, she touched his head and looked back down at Jeremy. "He's breathing but unconscious."

Jeremy shifted his weight, trying to balance on his left side because every step on his right sent a new jab of pain shooting up to his stomach. He looked down to see the new patch of blood soaking his shirt.

When he looked up again, a man stood at the top of the canyon, just outside the sedan, with his gun aimed right at Pax's prone form.

Jeremy shook his head in disbelief. So much for the idea he got the guy the first time.

Meredith didn't see the attacker and the guy didn't seem to notice Jeremy, which meant he retained the advantage. Forcing his hand to stop shaking, he aimed and pulled the trigger.

The shot thundered through the canyon as the man went down in a heap and Meredith threw her body over Pax.

When the air stilled again, her head shot up. She looked at the body a few feet from where she lay on Pax. Slowly her head turned and she faced Jeremy.

He forced his mouth to move. He smiled at her. "Got him."

Then he fell to his knees as everything around him went black. The last sound he heard was Meredith calling his name.

## Chapter Sixteen

Sara slipped out of the bathroom as soon as Meredith left. If Meredith could face whatever was happening without curling into a ball in the bathroom, Sara figured she could, too.

With her head held high, she crossed the big room to where the men were gathered around a chair. At the squeak of her sneaker against the floor, Garrett's head shot up. He treated her to a small shake of the head. She answered by ignoring him.

"Ms. Paulson." The older man in the suit, the guy who fit in the one-of-these-things-is-not-like-the-other category, noticed and acknowledged her. "It is nice to finally meet you."

She clearly was missing something because she'd never seen the guy before. Not ever. The younger version behind him was a stranger, too.

"Okay," she said, because she had no idea what else to say.

He approached her with his hand out. His cologne hit her the second before he touched her. She decided right then she preferred Garrett's earthy scent. It came from soap not a bottle, and that said something to her about the type of guy he was—all substance, no useless flash.

"I'm Ellis Martin."

She knew the name. Garrett didn't talk much about work, but he mentioned people. When he talked about Ellis, Garrett spoke with a begrudging respect. He also tended to swear a lot. Seemed Garrett and this guy were bound up in some kind of power struggle.

Sara decided that could only mean one thing. "You're Garrett's boss."

"And you're his fiancée."

She waited for Garrett to correct him. From the way Joel and Davis held their collective breaths, she guessed they were waiting for a denial, as well.

When none came, she decided to go with it. If Garrett wanted to keep their messed-up private life secret, she would oblige. The current state, whatever it was, didn't exactly reflect well on her anyway.

"Yes, I am."

Ellis bowed over her hand. For a second she thought he was going to kiss the back of it and thought about yanking it away. Instead, she gave his hand a tug and Ellis let go, but not before winking at her.

Garrett appeared at her side and his hand fell to her lower back, pulling her in tight to his side. The heat of his body engulfed her, and she sagged into him.

The whole show felt a bit heavy-handed. Not at all Garrett's usual style. While the whole "man's property" thing sure didn't appeal to her, something flip-flopped in her belly at the idea of him staking a claim.

A little emotion was all she ever wanted. A sign he viewed her as more than a box to check off as he ran through the list of things he should do with his life. She wanted to blame him for setting her bar so low, but she knew she had to take some responsibility. She'd accepted it. Well, she used to.

"This is my assistant, Andrew." Ellis nearly hit the

guy in the head during the no-eye-contact introduction. Andrew just nodded as he sat in the chair and turned on a laptop.

"We need a table," Ellis said.

Without another word, Davis disappeared into the bathroom and came out lugging a card table. He set it up then smacked the top. "Here you go."

Garrett's hand tightened on her back. "Why don't you—"

"No, she can stay." Ellis balanced a palm on the table and hovered over Andrew's shoulder. At Garrett's comment, he looked up. "You don't mind if Sara stays and watches us work, do you?"

Sara heard the challenge in Ellis's voice. Saw the battle play on Garrett's face as he fought off the urge to say he did mind.

"Of course not."

Since she was staying, she figured she might as well have a clue about what was going on. "What are we doing?"

"Facial recognition," Davis answered over the steady tap of Andrew's fingers against the keys.

"None of the attackers carried identification and we couldn't name them on sight." Garrett's frown eased as he talked. "We took photos and are running those through known databases to see if we get a match."

"You want to connect them to that Darren guy."

Garrett's eyes widened. "Yes."

She could only assume from the reaction that he didn't think she was smart enough to get the bottom line without a written paper on the subject. How flattering.

Ellis stared at his phone. After typing a few words, he dropped it back in his pocket. "I can't place any of them."

"Is that a problem?" she asked.

"Darren worked under me. Directly under Garrett, but in my section." Ellis's businesslike facade slipped and his hands balled into fists. "His access to hired guns should mirror mine."

Despite the tough-guy demeanor and a smile worthy of the smarmiest politician, his true feelings lurked under there. The punch of betrayal that crossed Garrett's face whenever he thought no one was looking also played for a few minutes on Ellis.

She reevaluated her decision not to trust him. "I assume the attackers were professionals."

Andrew glanced up at her, then went back to typing.

"We're guessing former military, possibly men who couldn't cut it." Ellis opened a file and pulled out a stack of photos. He spread them out on the table in a grid.

Garrett nodded. "There's a never-ending supply of disenchanted men willing to do whatever they have to do to earn some money."

"As long as they can carry a gun," Davis added.

Andrew didn't look up. "And get paid."

Sara glanced at the photos then vowed not to look again. "That's a scary thought."

"You should try sitting in my office. You wouldn't believe the depravity that crosses my desk." Ellis folded his arms across his chest, his boss attitude back in place.

Garrett cleared his throat. "And now imagine what it looks like in real life when you go one-on-one with this sort of trash."

All the sound sucked out of the room. Even Andrew stopped typing. Sara held her breath, waiting to see if the testosterone would overwhelm their good sense.

She wasn't in the mood to separate them. She had to do that sort of thing at the bridal shop now and then when nerves frayed and otherwise rational women resorted to a form of hair pulling, sometimes literally. She'd see mothers and daughters battle over everything from the cost of shoes to the dip of necklines.

A little pampering, a lot of champagne, and she could soothe most fragile and hyper dispositions. She doubted that tactic would work here.

After a few seconds, Ellis smiled. With an exaggerated bow, he turned to Garrett. "You win this round."

A breath hissed out between her lips. "Does the workday always go this way?"

Davis laughed. "Believe it or not, this is actually a good one."

"Ellis and I understand each other. He runs the business end. I run the operations." Garrett's lighter mood matched the rest of the room's. The change loosened the knot in her chest. For him to include her, let her see a tiny glimpse into his secret world, meant everything. Once this operation ended, she'd figure out a way to ask him to let her in. To keep the window cracked, if only a little.

"We should—" Ellis stood up with a frown full of what looked like genuine concern. "I'm sorry, Sara. Does it bother you to see these photos knowing the men are dead?"

She shook her head. "The men bothered me more when they were alive."

"I see why you're with Garrett." Ellis shot Garrett an unreadable look then went back to examining the photos.

The computer beeped and Sara was grateful she didn't have to respond.

"We have a match." Davis pointed to the screen.

They all gathered around Andrew's back. Joel, who had been so quiet during the entire exchange, read the name. "Rico Gabriel."

She looked around at the blank faces. "Who is that?"

"No idea," Ellis said. "Scroll down to aliases and known associates."

Sara scanned the list. One name popped out. She didn't know him, but she'd heard Jeremy mention him. The man who'd stabbed him.

"Bruce Casden." Joel's eyes narrowed. "So, this is about Jeremy?"

Garrett hadn't said anything. Hadn't moved.

Sara bit her lip. She ached for him and the pain she saw in his eyes. Her inclination was to wrap her arms around him and assure him Jeremy would be fine. But she hesitated, not wanting to be rejected or humiliate him in front of his men.

"Give me a phone." Garrett held out a hand and took the first cell he touched.

When he looked at her head-on, eyes blazing, her knees buckled. She knew for certain what she'd always suspected. Garrett would die for his brother. It was the right answer, and not a surprise, but the determination scared her to death.

He shifted the barest of inches and put his hand on her back. The touch radiated through her, wiping out some of her fears.

"It will be okay," she promised.

"I'm happy you're here."

# Chapter Seventeen

Meredith stared at the closed drapes. They were in adjoining rooms at the back of a three-story hotel on the way to the desert. Jeremy had taken roads she didn't even know existed and pulled off the highway in the sedan they'd stolen from their attacker. The path led to a simple place tucked between the mountains and run by one of Jeremy's informants.

Seeing the inside removed all her doubts. Clean sheets and big king beds piled high with pillows. Now she watched as Jeremy helped Pax out of the bathroom to the edge of the bed. Even balanced under Jeremy's arm, Pax's footsteps were unsure.

He sat down hard on the mattress. "I'm ready for this day to be over."

Meredith had basic first-aid training, but this situation needed more. They should be at a hospital, or at least with a doctor of some type. "You okay?"

Pax put a hand to his forehead and winced. "Except for the concussion."

"That settles it." She grabbed a towel and pointed toward the door. "We should go to the hospital."

"No," both men said at the same time.

"Gentlemen." She used her best teacher voice. "This is crazy."

"We barely made it here without becoming part of a canyon."

"Tell me how you think that furthers your argument."

Pax smiled through all the wincing. "She's got you there."

"We should all get checked out." She focused on Jeremy, hoping to get through to him before he bled out. "I saw the towels in the sink. You're bleeding again."

"It stopped."

Even Pax shot Jeremy a you've-got-to-be-kidding look at the denial.

Jeremy ignored the strange looks. "We're not going anywhere until we know it's safe to move. I'm done being chased and shot at. It's more dangerous in San Diego than at home."

The casual comment sliced through her. "Where is home?"

"Right now, Arizona." He threw out the answer like it was no big deal.

To her it meant something. She fought off the gnawing sense of loss. He was still here and already she missed him.

"We doubled back three times and covered our tracks. There's no way anyone can find us here," Jeremy said, as if trying to convince himself as well as them.

She hated to ask, but the question tickled at the back of her mind. "How do we know everyone is safe back at the garage?"

"I got the signal." His voice stayed steady as he said the words.

Which confused the crap out of her. "Tell me what that means in English."

"Garrett and I agreed to no communication. The plan

was if we were okay, I'd ping him. If all was fine there, he'd ping me back. I got the ping."

As far as she was concerned, he missed a pretty big problem with his theory. "Did you send a ping? Because the last few hours sure didn't feel okay to me. How do you know he isn't telling you what you want to hear to keep you from running back into danger?"

"I know." He didn't sound sure.

She used the tiny slip of doubt to push her point. "I think we should throw up the white flag and ask for help."

"I don't want them sending men into the same type of danger that we escaped. It's bad enough we came under fire. The team might not be lucky enough to survive a second time." Jeremy shook his head as he walked away from the bed. "No, they stay where they are, with Ellis's Secret Service detail there to add firepower."

Jeremy had opened the door to this conversation, so she breezed right through. "Then will you at least admit that you've had this operation all wrong from the start?"

Pax whistled as he propped his head on the pillow stack. "That's a gutsy lady right there."

Jeremy's narrow-eyed frown suggested otherwise. "What are you talking about?"

"You are the target. Not Garrett. You." Since he didn't look convinced, she laid out her argument, ticking off each point on her fingers. "The Coronado house was in a corporation in both your names. The attacker followed us, not Garrett."

"That doesn't mean—"

"You were stabbed and your work is just as dangerous as your brother's. There is a man sitting in prison waiting for you to testify. Darren isn't the only one."

"Go on."

At least it wasn't a rabid denial. She hoped that was a

good sign. "It is conceivable the revenge is against you. That you are the one in danger. From where I sit, it's more likely than the Darren–Garrett scenario."

Pax looked at her through one open eye. "She has some good points."

She gave one more push. "Maybe you should tell us what happened on your last job to give you that slice in your side."

Jeremy glanced at Pax, who had nodded off in midsentence. "We should let Pax rest."

"Should he?"

"His vision is fine. No blurriness. He doesn't have nausea. We have to watch him, but we can check in every hour."

She bit her lower lip. "What if something happens, like it's more serious, and we could have prevented it by being in the hospital?"

"I've had a concussion before. That's the standard treatment."

She let Jeremy steer her into the other bedroom. When he closed the connecting door, her heart started flipping around. Close proximity and a bed. Sounded like a dangerous combination to her.

She turned around and spied him. He stood with his back to the door and his hand on the doorknob. He didn't look scared or worried…not exactly. But something unsure lurked there.

"Bruce Casden stabbed me when he figured out I was an agent. Until then, I was a budding player in his operation."

"What kind of operation?" She wanted to go to Jeremy but suspected he didn't want any tenderness right now.

He needed to get the words out, regardless of how painful they were. Dragging them out of him struck her as a horrible way to spend the evening, but trapping them inside was destroying him.

"Drugs. He runs them, sells them and sneaks them into the country through drug trafficking tunnels that stretch from Mexico to businesses he owns and likes to pretend are legitimate. He's been under investigation for years but always managed to slither away."

"You were undercover." The past year fell together in her head. He'd been out and hunted. She'd been hanging out in a classroom and playing tenant.

She loved her life, but his work made parts of it seem shallow. Not the kids, but the other stuff. The silly girl stuff.

"I got in through his girlfriend." The storms brewing inside him halted his speech and had him shuffling his feet. "Befriended her when I tended bar in the club where she sang."

"And Bruce eventually found out it was all a sham."

"She was in on it. She wanted out of that life. I let her believe…" Jeremy let his head fall back against the door with a crack. "She thought we were together. That I would whisk her away and keep her safe."

Meredith hated hearing this part. The days when he cared for someone else sent her self-confidence spiraling down. "You wanted to."

"That's the sick part. I viewed her as a job." He pushed away from the door and came over to sit next to her on the bed.

His words punched and pricked at Meredith. She kept her expression blank, not wanting him to stop talking. It was like a streaming poison and he needed it out of his system.

"I would have taken her out of the building, away from Bruce's reach, and dumped her right in witness protection. I would have told myself I was helping, because that's what I've done before, but really my goal was to hurt Bruce in every way I could. Stealing his woman assured that." Jeremy let out a noise somewhere between a yell and a growl. "That's the great guy I am."

Meredith slid her hand between Jeremy's palms and looped her other arm over his shoulders. "You are."

He finally faced her. "You're not getting it. I set her up."

She'd understood every word. In some ways, she thought she got the parts he didn't. "You would have stepped in."

"You don't know that. I can't guarantee that."

"I know exactly what you'd do in this situation. You could have run, leaving me with the police to answer all the questions about the fire. But you didn't."

Every act he'd taken since they left Coronado fell into place. It all made sense. She was the woman he could save.

The idea of being the makeup for past sins crushed her. All her hopes and girlish fantasies of seeing him after they got out of this mess vanished in a huge exploding poof.

"He killed her and stabbed me. Cut me and watched while I lay bleeding on the floor." The harsh words came out in a tone that sounded as if it were rubbed with gravel.

There it was. The horrible punch line to the nightmare he'd been living. She'd known the twisting, terrible truth was coming, but the words slashed through her anyway.

"A fellow agent saved me. We'd made arrangements to meet about Serena, and when I didn't show he sent everyone in firing. Finding me on the floor made it tough for Bruce to buy off judges. He was caught in the act for the first time. When I lived to talk about the tunnels, it was all over for him."

Jeremy squeezed her hand between his. "So you see, Bruce has a reason to want me dead. I took everything from him. I'm the one who put him in jail and I will keep him there no matter what I need to do to make it happen."

She wasn't sure what to make of that comment. But she did recognize guilt when she saw it. "What was her name?"

"Serena." He dropped his head into his hands. "She's buried in a ditch off an abandoned road. Or she was until the police took the sniffer dogs and all the equipment and dug her up again."

It sounded so dehumanizing. So cruel. "I'm sorry."

"The idea that I dropped this violence at your door. And Sara, who has no clue what to do with what's happening around her. It's just sick."

Meredith snorted. Man, they all played the same game with Sara. The poor thing must spend all her time convincing her loved ones she'd grown up. Meredith had tasted that with her own parents and it was a terrible way to live.

"Sara is tougher than you think, and she needs to get used to this life and all its dangers since she's marrying your brother."

"You sure about that?"

"Yes. As soon as he figures out the wedding dress saleswoman wants a real wedding they'll be fine. She wanted him back. He just needs to work a little bit." Meredith rolled her eyes. "Honestly, he is so slow."

"I don't know what any of that means."

"And that makes me nervous."

"What?"

"Never mind."

Jeremy fell back on the bed and she followed him down. He needed someone to soothe and control him.

He'd fight it. He'd deny the need, but she wanted to give it as much as he needed to receive it.

She curled her arm on his chest as she balanced her head on her hand and stared down at him. "What do we do now?"

"I have a scheduled check-in with Garrett in about—" Jeremy reached over and turned the bedside clock to face him "—thirty minutes."

"Maybe in the meantime we could have that next date? I believe you promised me something a bit less dangerous this time. If the bad guys hold off, we should be able to work it in."

She sounded flip, but in reality, what she suggested was the risk of a lifetime. She couldn't stop her heart from taking the trip.

He lifted his head. "What are you saying?"

"Clearly my girl powers are misfiring."

"After what I just told you about me, about my life, you want to be with me?" His voice said no but his breathing picked up speed.

She dragged her hand down his chest and tunneled under his T-shirt to hit bare skin. "Was I supposed to hear all the facts and hate you? Be disgusted?"

"Why not? I am." Such harsh words while his fingers brushed gentle strokes in her hair.

"You know what I see when I look at you?" He opened his mouth to answer and she cut him off. She dreaded what he might say while he wallowed in his guilt. "A man who loves his brother. A man who puts others before himself. A rescuer. A good man, flawed but real."

"I killed her, Meredith. I didn't pull the trigger, but my actions put her in the ground."

"She wanted out. She knew the risks."

"It's not that simple."

Meredith sighed as she worked up the nerve she needed to say the words. "Serena picked Bruce in the first place. The one thing I've learned is that, regardless of how awful the guy is, if you date him, move in with him, marry him, you have to take some of the responsibility for your bad decision to stay with him."

"You didn't ask to be abused."

"No, but I allowed Clint to break me down and part of that is on me, just as Serena's decisions—good and bad—are on her."

"Meredith." Jeremy lifted his shoulders off the bed and kissed her.

The skimming of his lips over hers wiped away every bad choice and every sad hour. The craving for him didn't lessen. He got near her and it flamed. He touched his mouth to hers and her insides caught fire.

Rolling, he tucked her under him and took the kiss even deeper. Heat, mouth, hands. The mix sent her temperature spiraling and her doubts crashing to the floor.

She grabbed the bottom of his shirt and tugged until it slipped up his arms and off him. While it floated to the floor, she gave in to her desire to kiss and touch that firm chest.

A rip of a zipper drowned out their heavy breathing and soft pleas to go faster. The denim brushed down her legs. He lifted off her then returned to press his weight onto her.

Her fingers traveled down his stomach until they hit the top of his bandage. Somewhere in the back of her head an alarm bell dinged.

She broke off the crushing kiss. "Are you okay to do this?"

"You're asking that now?" He sounded stunned at her timing.

When he ducked his head to kiss the top of her breast, she pushed against him. "I'm serious."

"Are you really worried about this?" He was panting as need clouded his eyes.

She slipped her hand under his waistband, knowing her words and her actions collided in ways that didn't make much sense. "I don't want to rupture your—"

He captured her mouth and rolled her back over. When she lifted her head, her legs straddled his waist and his back rested against the mattress. "Better?"

She could hear the laughter in his voice.

When she sat up, he groaned. His erection pressed against her and his hands fell to her hips.

At the intimate touch her brain went fuzzy. "Condom?"

"One in my pocket."

Not the answer she expected. "Really?"

"Pax and Davis brought it when they dropped off the clothes…whenever that was. Days ago? It's all blending." His hands slipped over her stomach and his thumb dipped lower. "Do we have to talk about this now?"

One, two, three, he brushed against her through her panties. Her body melted as her breath came on soft pants. Happiness bubbled up inside her when she saw the look of wonder on his face as he watched his hand move over her.

She leaned down and kissed him then. Sighed when she felt him unclip her bra and slip his palms around to cup her breasts. While his hands toured her body, she slipped her fingers in his pocket and pulled out the packet.

The move put her flat against him, bare chest to bare chest. "You feel so good against me," he mumbled against her neck.

"Yes." Every inch of her fit snug and perfect against him.

When he tugged at her shirt, she sat up and stripped

it off. Those blue eyes wandered over her skin as a smile
fell across his lips. "Beautiful."

"This is a much better date."

His hand slipped behind her neck and brought her
closer. "One favor?"

She'd give him just about anything if he kissed her
again. "Sure."

"Ride me."

## Chapter Eighteen

Bruce paced the confines of his cell. The walls closed in tighter today than usual.

He'd been waiting for a status check-in for hours. The two calls to his lawyer had gone unanswered. No one had picked up to accept the collect call.

Stephen had disobeyed one too many times. Bruce detested insubordination, especially when it came from pseudo-powerful men who forgot their places. Bruce would remind him.

Firing him would be too easy. Finding a new lawyer would only push back the timing of his case and send the wrong message to the already tight-fisted judge.

No, Bruce decided to punish Stephen in a way he would remember. Give him pain only the two of them would know was self-inflicted. After all, how hard could it be to arrange for the "accidental" overdose of a college kid with access to too much cash?

But first Bruce needed to know what was happening. Killing Jeremy fed a need inside Bruce. It also satisfied his thirst for revenge. Most importantly, it put him one giant step closer to getting out of a cell and back to his life.

Then he'd turn his attention to the prosecutor. Take out Garrett Hill to complete the revenge. There was no need

Bruce could see for either Hill brother to live. At least, not when Bruce had already decided to kill the women.

Steady footsteps sounded from the far end of the cell block. The pattern never changed. The guard started at one end, the same end, and walked to the other. He'd stop once or twice. Bang his nightstick against the bars to make sure he had everyone's attention.

Bruce ticked off the pattern in his head until the footsteps slowed outside his cell. He waited for a note to drop to the floor.

*Nothing.*

The guard reached the far end of the cell and turned. Bruce saw the facial profile. Saw the slight shake of his head.

His blood burned through his veins. His inside man had broken contact. He'd better have a very good excuse or he'd be sharing a hole in the dirt with Jeremy.

JEREMY CLIMBED OUT of bed, careful not to shake the mattress or wake Meredith. He had to check on Pax, but that didn't mean he couldn't spare a minute to stare at her.

She was the woman he'd never asked for and always assumed didn't exist. She'd seen violence and rather than cave in, she thrived. Because of him she'd been dragged all over San Diego County—with a gun pointed at her head most of the time—with no explanations, and she'd never balked.

And the sex was pure fire. If he could even call it sex. Hot and sweaty. All hands and mouths, legs and arms. But there was a spark of something else there, too. Something deep and important, and because it scared the shit out of him he pushed it out of his head.

Conquering fear and facing violence required strength. Walking willingly into it, inviting it into your life on a daily basis, required a different level of commitment and more than a little bit of a death wish. For the first time he understood Garrett's desperation about losing Sara and being left alone, even as he feared he would destroy her.

Jeremy wanted Meredith safe but he wanted her with him, and those two things just didn't fit together.

His gaze bounced back to her long hair spread over the pillow. Her body, from her long legs to those knowing hands, wrapped around what was his pillow. The lady was a cuddler. With a body like that, he didn't complain. She could lie all over him any time she wanted.

One tanned leg peeked out from under the white sheet. Those pink toenails. He'd spent a lot of time admiring the color as he kissed every inch of her.

Much more of this and he'd be climbing back into bed and ignoring Pax's head. Before Jeremy could weigh those options and put Pax at greater risk without good reason, he tore his gaze away from her. He scanned the floor for his pants, figuring Pax wouldn't appreciate a naked guy hovering over him calling his name.

The jeans lay in a pile on the floor. Jeremy had no idea how they got... Oh, that's right. He smiled at the memory of her dragging the pants down his legs. That one would stay with him for a very long time. Probably had something to do with the fact she was naked at the time.

He picked the jeans up and turned them around to double-check for another condom. A guy could hope. Since Pax was good enough to include the first, it was worth a try.

The bump under Jeremy's fingertip had him pulling the pants closer for an inspection. At first he thought it was some type of store security tag, but the shape and size were wrong.

He rubbed and picked until the black dot came off in

his hand. A closer look told him exactly what he needed to know and probably should have suspected. A tracking device. Small but effective. The bad guys knew where to race them off the road because they knew where Jeremy was at all times.

Bruce didn't have this sort of technology. Despite his belief that he ran a huge operation, he was a loser who couldn't find a real job so he turned to the easier occupation of drug runner.

Jeremy closed his hand, prepared to crush the device. Then he opened his fingers again.

*Think.*

Bruce might not know computers, but he had the money to pay off people who did. One of those people sat in a garage with his brother right now. Only a few people knew every move and could try to cut them all off with gunfire. The list narrowed significantly when it came to the last attack. The person had to depend on the tracker, which meant Jeremy knew who it was. A man who'd had one opportunity to plant the device.

Without rustling the curtains or causing any visible sign of movement that could be seen outside, he peeked out the window. The night remained quiet.

Jeremy squinted to get a better look. The only difference was the presence of two cars sitting up the road. Two black sedans that resembled the one Jeremy borrowed.

They were here and setting up, likely waiting for the right opportunity to move. When they attacked, he'd be in trouble because Pax couldn't hold his head up and Meredith shouldn't have to fight. Her stamina surpassed his, but she still wasn't an expert. Logging in hours at the shooting range didn't change that.

That meant Jeremy needed a new plan. One that would end this and draw out the mole. The only question was—

how many people would die in the process? He didn't have anyone on his side he was willing to sacrifice.

Except the mole.

He grabbed his cell and slipped into the bathroom, but left the door open a crack in case Meredith needed him. Since he kept staring at her, he knew which one of them was needy.

Garrett picked up on the first ring. Jeremy launched into his speech before Garrett said a word. "I'm texting you our location. We need a plan to flush out the mole. I think I know who it is, but it's going to be dangerous."

As if that ever mattered to him.

He glanced at Meredith's bare leg again. Followed the line of her body to the side of her sweet face.

For some reason, it mattered now.

## Chapter Nineteen

"Is everything okay?" Sara waited to ask Garrett until they were alone and crowded together over the tiny sink.

Ever since he'd answered the last call, he'd been jumpy. Not that other people would notice. No, on the surface he maintained his smooth control. She saw the cracking lines in the worried stares into nothing and constant tugging at his ear.

Instead of standing beside her, he rested his palms against the counter, trapping her between them with his chest pressed to her back. When she tried to turn around, he lowered his face to her hair.

"We have a plan."

She froze at the sound of his whisper. She didn't ask if this new plot was dangerous, because almost everything he did was. "What can I do?"

"I'll need your acting skills."

She turned in his arms then and stared into those blue eyes she loved so much. "How do you know I have any?"

"You told me you were in plays in high school."

She'd mentioned it once in passing while he read the paper. She never would have guessed he heard her. "So, I'm part of the plan?"

"An integral part."

"This is a first."

"You're not the only one who's learned something about us."

Her breath caught in her throat and held there. She dared to hope. "What did you learn?"

"That I can trust you. I should have known it all the time, but—"

"You were slow."

"That's the Coronado thing." He reached down and took her hand in his, pressing tiny kisses along each knuckle. "I'm sorry. I'll spend forever trying to make it up to you."

His gaze met hers and held. The promise she saw there filled her with a giddiness she could barely contain.

But he needed to know she now had boundaries. "Just don't lie to me again. Don't shut me out."

Instead of making his usual excuses and changing the subject, he nodded. "You're in."

He kissed her. His mouth lingered and the heat built. He chuckled when he pulled back. "Now probably isn't the time, though it kills me to say that."

She stepped out of his arms, thinking some space might put them back in a work mood. "Are you going to brief all of us?"

"The only ones who know about this will be you and Ellis."

"Ellis?" Not the name she was expecting.

"I need his men."

But that didn't explain the obvious question. "Why me?"

"Because there's no one I trust more in the world than you."

A sudden lightness burst through her. He finally said the right thing.

THE CARS ARRIVED at dawn, just like Jeremy said they would. In a weird nod to forgetting all signs of secrecy, the team piled out of the SUVs, talking but staying together in a tight formation as they headed for the opposite side of the building.

The only people missing were the Secret Service agents. Meredith wondered how Jeremy had managed that.

The men surrounded Sara, and the two suits from Garrett's agency had also joined in the fun. The scowl on Garrett's face could stop a man's heart. He'd tried to keep Sara out of this side of his life and now she was all up in it. Meredith couldn't imagine what that did to his sense of balance.

Davis turned and aimed his keys at the van. The alarm chirped. Yeah, nothing silent about this entrance.

Meredith shook her head, wondering if this was what happened when a man came up with a plan after sex. Very strange. Not what she'd seen from Jeremy so far.

A noise behind her had Meredith spinning around. Jeremy came out with a towel wrapped around his waist and another hanging around his neck. Her body flushed from the sight of him as that giddy buzz hit her head.

Her gaze touched on his chest and all the other places her mouth had explored the night before. Sara's words came back like a lightning bolt. It was far too easy to fall for a Hill brother.

"What do you think?" he asked as he lifted his chin and turned his head from side to side.

The new haircut threw her off for a second. Jeremy now wore a military cut identical to his brother's. The severe style made Jeremy seem older, more stiff. Something about his previous scruffier look had fit his personality. She half expected this version to start issuing orders.

"That's just weird." She ran her fingers over the top, missing the soft strands that had fallen through her fingers last night.

After a quick kiss, he threw the towel from around his neck to the chair by the bathroom. "The point is to fool the bad guys."

He tossed the argument off. To him it probably meant nothing, but she wanted to be sure he saw himself as she did.

"Your identity is about more than your haircut. It starts in here." She touched her palm to her heart. "And travels to here." She tapped his head.

After all those hours of pillow talk, he still didn't understand who he was, separate from the badge and the birthright.

He wiggled his eyebrows. "There are other body parts you could touch."

"Behave." The order died when she smiled. She couldn't help it. Happiness flooded through her today.

Her emotions yo-yoed. One minute she thought they could try something without the threat of danger. Other times she knew to her soul this was the only time they'd have and she should treasure it.

"And for the record, you can tell the difference between me and Garrett. You and Sara." He let his arms fall loose around her waist. "The bad guys will just see hair and react to that."

"You're awfully calm even though the guys you're talking about are right outside and loaded down with weapons."

"They have been since we got here." He kissed the base of her throat.

She shoved against his shoulders until he pulled back and looked at her. "What?"

"I saw them last night when I went to check on Pax."

One more secret added to all the others. "Why didn't you wake me?"

"I knew they weren't going to strike. They want me and Garrett together. They needed him to get here first."

"So, naturally, you brought your brother here."

His hands traveled down to her butt and lifted her until her body fit snug against his. "It's going to be fine. You need to trust me on this."

She knew he'd hate this part, but she had to say it. "Promise me you won't take any unnecessary risks. No throwing your body in front of other people or diving to take a bullet meant for a stray dog."

He gave her a look that let her know what he thought of her exaggeration. "Meredith, I have a plan."

"So you keep saying."

He sobered. "No matter what happens, I need you to know I'm fine."

"That's just cryptic enough to make me uncomfortable." Maybe she would have accepted that a week ago. Now she expected the comment to accompany a round of gunfire.

Pretty funny for a woman who'd spent every minute of her life since she'd fallen down the stairs insisting she'd never experience violence again.

"I need my pants." He tapped her bottom then went looking.

"I guess I can't convince you to jump in a car with me and run away from here."

He shot her a look over his shoulder. "You know I can't."

"I do. Yes."

His turn back to her was slow. "Meaning?"

"Next time you launch into a lecture about how terrible you are, remember this moment. When everything is on the line, including your safety, you rush in. You're that guy."

"What do you think about 'that guy' exactly?"

"I'll tell you after you finish this operation and actually get that rest you were ordered to take."

His grin could have broken records. "Deal."

LESS THAN FIFTEEN minutes later, the whole team met in a small conference room on the first floor.

Jeremy scanned each of them, looking for any sign he'd tagged the wrong guy. The usual tells—sweating, talking fast, fidgeting—were absent. The collective years of training in the room got them beyond those basics.

No, if the mole was here, and Jeremy knew he was, he'd blend in. He'd cause the damage then weasel out without anyone ever knowing he'd been there.

Everyone took their positions, including the women, without complaint or tipping anyone off to a problem. The rumble of conversation added to the steady buzz of activity. Every person had a job and was doing it.

"Andrew?" Jeremy called out to the younger man and wasn't surprised when the order made the guy jump. "You can set up over there and let us know if anyone breaches a fifty-yard safety zone around the building."

"Yes, sir." He slipped his laptop onto the desk and started typing.

"Are we the only ones in the hotel?" Sara asked.

"Yes, I even sent the manager out to be safe."

Joel slipped into a green conference chair. "What makes you so sure anyone will come?"

He looked at Garrett as he asked, as if challenging him to make an accusation. Garrett ignored him and concentrated on his phone instead.

"I can answer that." Ellis rounded the head of the table with a mug of coffee in his hand. He put his suit jacket on the back of the chair in one of the more obvious shows of territory marking. "Because Bruce wants Jeremy dead. He's launched several attacks so far. He's betting this one will work."

"I don't get it." Joel shook his head. "He has to know the spotlight will be on him if this happens. And he has to get through all of us first. Why take the risk?"

"Does he really have anything to lose?" Davis asked.

"Remember that Jeremy didn't even think he was the target until an hour or so ago. There are a lot of enemies out there. It could take months to get to the right one. If Bruce were smart, by then he'd be gone." Garrett pointed at his phone. "Jeremy, are you getting this on your end?"

He took out his phone and punched a few buttons to bring up a video. "Looks like we have a problem."

"What?" Panic rumbled through Meredith's voice. She was at his side before he could draw his next breath.

"Don't worry," he said. "Pax and Davis will stay with you. Joel, you come with us."

Shock sprinted across Joel's face, but he tamped it back down. "Of course."

Meredith stepped in front of Jeremy when he tried to leave. "You can't go running off somewhere. You promised me."

Her fingernails dug into his arms as she pleaded with him to stay. The pain he saw on her face ate at him. He wanted to explain, to reassure her, but all those opportunities were gone. Now he was stuck with moving her to the side so he could get going and hoping she'd understand later.

He leaned down and kissed her. In front of everyone and without a lick of privacy, he took her mouth and

treated her to a knee-buckling kiss. When he raised hi
head again, her lips were swollen and her eyes unfocusec

He bolted. He was out the door when he heard he
calling after him. To keep walking, he had to block th
sound. He'd hear it again, probably as she yelled at hir
again, but he had to do this first.

Garrett scowled at his brother as he walked down th
hall toward the exit. "What took you so long?"

"Meredith."

Some of Garrett's frown eased. "Women."

The Hill brothers laughed, but Joel stayed quiet as h
followed Garrett and Jeremy into the sunshine and out
the garages behind the hotel. The three of them steppe
into a large empty room.

Jeremy walked the length of the space and tested th
cabinets at the far end. Everything was right where
should be. When he paid his informant Jeremy woul
add extra this time.

Joel stopped in the dead center of the room. "What a
we doing here? This doesn't make any sense."

Jeremy got his brother's attention and nodded.

"We have some information we need to discuss." Ga
rett made the announcement in an angry voice. "Anythir
you want to say first?"

"You still don't trust me." Joel turned away from Ga
rett to stare at a blank space on the wall. "This is unbe
lievable."

Garrett came up behind him. This time he lowere
his voice. "You're with us because I do. It's not going
seem that way, but I do."

Joel spun around. "I don't—"

"Go to the window. Do not believe what you see."

Joel shook his head. "You're not making any sense."

Jeremy knew the kid was right on the edge. He wa

going to blow the plan by doing the job he was paid to do—question and verify. This was why Jeremy begged his brother to cut Joel in. They'd needed Ellis's help to gather the men. Garrett insisted the trust line end there, and now they had an even bigger mess.

To keep from sending them all down the road into real disaster, Jeremy morphed into bad cop. He stalked over and grabbed Joel by the neck, shaking him while he yelled. "You heard your boss."

"Do not touch me." Joel kicked and fought. He even got in a shot or two, which had Jeremy swearing and dodging. But he didn't let go.

He leaned in with his face right next to Joel's ear and said the magic words. "When the time comes, tell them one dead. One almost dead. We trust you to do this."

Joel stopped thrashing around.

The banging started a second later.

Jeremy shoved Joel to the far wall as the walls exploded with gunfire. Splintered wood flew through the air. Light streamed through the pattern of holes in the walls.

Shouts and screams echoed in the distance as Joel dropped to the ground. Jeremy fell into Garrett. The packets passed from one hand to the other.

With a snap, Jeremy broke the package. Going down in a hail of fake bullets, he wiped the "blood" over himself and let the rest of the packet drop to the floor. By the time they landed on their stomachs on the ground, red liquid pooled around them.

After a minute, the intense banging stopped, leaving the building to creak and moan as the remaining structure fought to stay standing.

The door opened and a woman screamed in a sound so full of anguish and pain that Pax covered his ears. They all stood in stunned horror as Joel rushed over to the Hill brothers, sliding across the floor to reach them first.

"Keep them back and look for the shooters." Wood crunched under his knees as Joel moved around the bodies.

"Let me help." Pax rushed in ready to offer medical assistance.

Joel sat back. "One dead. One about there."

"I'll do CPR."

Joel caught Pax's hands before he could touch the bodies. "Call an ambulance."

## Chapter Twenty

Meredith stumbled around in a helpless daze. She'd walked the hospital floor about a hundred times since the ambulance had brought Garrett and Jeremy in. With every step she tried to wipe away the memory of the bloodbath.

Streaks of red across the floor. More bullet holes than she'd ever seen at a practice range. Bruce's men had opened fire as Garrett and Jeremy talked. All the technology had failed. All the promises of being safe and coming back rang hollow.

She'd tried to fall over Jeremy and push some life into his still body but Ellis had closed in. His men, absent when the world exploded, poured in after. With talk of crime-scene evidence, the men pushed them all out then loaded Garrett and Jeremy into the ambulance in a rush.

She didn't even get to see Jeremy's face. She had no idea which brother Joel had pronounced dead.

Her eyes burned from all the tears. She looked around the private waiting room on the floor Ellis had cleared of other patients. Amazing what the right government badge could do. If only he had stepped up earlier.

Pax and Davis talked in hushed tones in the corner. Andrew paced and managed to look concerned even though he didn't know anyone in the room except Ellis.

Sara sat in a chair with her arms wrapped around herself and rocked.

The only person missing from the group was Joel. Secret Service had carted him away as he protested and proclaimed his innocence.

Meredith choked back the bile in her throat. She'd believed him. Stuck up for him. Her stupidity had led the brothers to slaughter.

Another time when she'd read a man wrong. This time it might cost her everything. The idea of Jeremy dying had her sobbing. She coughed to hide the sound. She had to be strong. She could fall apart later.

A doctor stepped into the room. His blue scrubs were stained with red and a grim line ran across his mouth.

Ellis met the doctor before he could search the room for family members. "How are they?"

The doctor shook his head. Every slip from right to left cut away a piece of her. Her coffee cup dropped from her hand. The hot liquid splashed against her legs but she didn't feel it.

"We lost one. He was dead when he arrived. There was nothing we could do."

Meredith heard a cry. A long scream that sounded like *no*. She looked around and realized everyone was looking at her.

Pax rushed to her side. "I got you."

"He can't be dead." A shocking numbness settled over her body.

"Let's sit down." He put her in a seat then sat next to her.

His arm was around her and the cool air blasted from the air-conditioning vents, but nothing touched her. She closed her eyes and saw Jeremy captured in a deathly stillness. She opened them and the nightmare continued.

"We've stabilized the other brother, but he's in critical condition," the doctor said without any emotion. "The next few hours will tell. If he makes it until tomorrow morning, the chances are good he'll survive."

The word propelled her to her feet. Pax made a grab for her but she squirmed out of his hands. She pushed through the crowd and reached for the doctor's arm. "Why aren't you using their names?"

"What?"

"Who is dead? Which one?" The answer would devastate one woman in the room and save the other.

The doctor cleared his voice and glanced at Ellis before continuing. "That's the problem. They're identical. We don't know."

The comment didn't make any sense. She knew. Sara certainly knew.

Meredith reached for Sara, dragging her out of her seat to stand with her in front of the doctor. "She can tell them apart. Tell them."

"Stop." Sara dug in her heels and skidded across the floor. "I can't."

The words hit Meredith like a slap. She turned on Sara. "You know the face of the man you love."

Sara kept shaking her head. Her vacant eyes wouldn't meet Meredith's. "Don't ask me to go in there."

Meredith shook her. "How can you sit out here and not need to know?"

Ellis was on her a second later. Firm hands wrapped around her upper arms and pulled her off Sara. "Meredith, enough. Everyone is upset."

Meredith shook her head. She was willing to do anything to shake life back into her dying body. "Is this you upset? You're barely breathing."

The doctor motioned for someone. "I can sedate—"

"Don't touch me."

She screamed the phrase over and over until the world went black.

ELLIS WALKED OUT of the hospital room and ran right into Andrew.

No surprise there.

The younger man stopped pacing and stared at his boss. "How is he?"

Ellis wiped a hand through his hair, wondering how much more they could all take of this. Sara looked ready to crack and they'd put Meredith out to keep control over her.

But Ellis knew his role. "The real question is, who is he? Which brother is it?"

On cue, Andrew frowned in concern. "You really can't tell?"

"No."

"Huh." Andrew made a clicking sound with his tongue.

Ellis fought the urge to punch the little punk in the face. "What is it?"

"Would an objective look help? I mean, I don't have a vested interest. It could be you want to see Jeremy and are blinded by that."

And the trap was sprung.

"I'm willing to try anything." Ellis walked him inside.

Equipment beeped and lights flashed. A body, Garrett or Jeremy, Ellis didn't even know which, lay in the bed wrapped in stillness.

Andrew paled at the sight of the bandages and machinery. "How is he going to survive this?"

"The doctor thinks there's a good chance because both brothers were, are, heck I don't know which term is right, in such good shape. They put him in a medical coma and are helping him breathe."

"That's good news."

Ellis's phone beeped and he pretended to read a message. "I'll be right back."

Jeremy couldn't see anything but he heard the footsteps. From the conversation around him, he knew Andrew stood by the machine that supposedly pumped air and kept the patient alive. Something ripped and the air stopped flowing.

Wheels creaked as they rolled across the floor, taking the nearby cart with them, and the needle in his arm popped out. A buzz filled the room as Andrew lowered the top portion of the bed to put Jeremy flat.

It was going to be pure joy to rip this guy's life apart. He was trading his integrity for cash, and Jeremy didn't care what happened to him.

Hot breath spilled across Jeremy's cheek and he fought back the need to move.

"Which brother are you, I wonder. Of course it doesn't matter. Bruce Casden wants you both dead." Buttons clicked and the last whir of the equipment in the room fell silent as Andrew talked. "My only regret is that I only get to kill one of you. Casden's people beat me to the other one."

The bed dipped but Jeremy forced every muscle to remain still, every breath to seep in slowly.

"Everyone was looking in the wrong place for me. I infiltrated Ellis's office to get one brother and eventually the other. Casden has a message for you...." Andrew leaned in even closer. "He wishes he was here to see you die."

*Now.*

Jeremy's eyes popped open. Just in time, too. Andrew held a pillow in the air, just above Jeremy's face.

"Anything else Bruce wanted me to know?" Jeremy asked.

Andrew fell back, his mouth comically wide as a scream rattled out of him. "You're dead!"

"Tell Bruce I'm fine." Jeremy swung his legs over the side of the bed and grabbed the pillow from Andrew. "Shouldn't be a problem since you'll be sharing a cell."

"Unless I kill him first." Ellis delivered his comment from the doorway with Garrett standing right behind him.

Andrew's eyes darted. He looked like the cornered rat he was. "Both of you? But…I… One of you is dead."

"Wrong." Jeremy took pleasure in saying the word.

Andrew shook his head. "You've got this all mixed up. It isn't what you think."

"Neither was the shooting." Garrett smiled. "Funny how, if you ask a few Secret Service guys if they want to dress up and shoot, they jump on the chance to join in the game."

Jeremy filled Andrew in on the other big part of the plan. "They grabbed your guys, or should I say Bruce's guys, first."

Andrew shook his head. "This is a mistake."

When he reached for his pocket, Jeremy wrestled the other man's hands behind his back. Might have tugged a bit harder than needed, too. "You did that clumsy routine and planted the tracker. You turned off my life-saving machines. I took that as a sign you wanted me dead."

"What I don't get is, why?" Ellis moved in front of his former assistant. "You had a career. A family with money. But you get involved with a creep like Bruce Casden."

Garrett snorted. "Money. It's always about money."

The terror in Andrew's face morphed into disgust. He spat at Ellis. "You've always been so stupid."

Ellis just smiled. "I'm not the one going to jail."

"Listening to you drone on every day made me want to kill you, too." The shaky nervousness in Andrew's voice vanished. Now he spoke with a steady venom that cracked like a whip. "You don't get it. None of you. Bruce Casden has power. Real power. He'll beat this like he has every other charge."

Jeremy pretended to mull the comment over. "He might. You won't. Trying to kill a federal agent?"

Garrett frowned and shook his head with a hefty dose of dramatics. "That's major time."

"I won't spend one day in jail."

"Right. You'll spend thirty years. And a pretty boy like you." Ellis picked up a towel and wiped the spit off his shirt. "I hope it was worth it."

Jeremy's patience expired. "Get him out of here."

TWENTY MINUTES LATER Jeremy was back in his clothes and the team filed into his room. He turned to Ellis. "Thanks for lending us your guys."

"They enjoyed having a chance to shoot at Garrett here, even if it was with fake bullets."

Jeremy's gaze went to Joel. "You okay?"

Joel nodded. "Yeah."

The harsh lines had faded from his face. Ghosts still moved through him as he separated himself from the group physically, but Jeremy hoped Garrett could lure him back to the team. The frowns on the faces of Davis and Pax looked less promising. When Jeremy turned to them, they stepped out into the hall.

The move made Jeremy stop for a second. He had no idea what the cut meant, but he wanted to make sure Joel got it. "We brought you in because we knew you weren't the mole."

"But we used the fact other people did to give Andrew an added sense of security." Garrett kept his arm locked around Sara's waist as he talked.

The closeness made Jeremy smile. Somehow his idiot brother had fixed his relationship mess. But the touching and warm smiles made him miss the one person he wanted in the room. "Where's Meredith?"

Ellis backed up a step. "Down the hall."

Jeremy's heart pounded hard enough to muffle the conversation. He had to concentrate to get the words out. "She's in a room here?"

Ellis looked to Garrett before continuing. "We had to knock her out."

Jeremy's brain went blank. "What?"

"Seems the lady really cares for you." Ellis smoothed the lapel of his jacket as he shifted out of Jeremy's grabbing range.

Sara didn't suffer from the same fear. She stepped up until she stood right in front of her future brother-in-law. "I can't believe you didn't tell her the truth."

The vehemence in Sara's voice stunned Jeremy as much as the conversation. "Garrett told you?"

"He didn't want me to worry."

"You're alive." Meredith's shaky voice stopped all conversation. They all turned and looked at her standing in the doorway in the hospital scrubs.

Jeremy saw the wild eyes and hands balled into fists and his heart sank. He'd done this to her. He'd put her in the middle of an unbelievable situation and ripped her apart.

He reached out to her but she smacked his hands away.

Her glare traveled the room as she stood there. "You all knew?"

"Only Ellis and Sara." Garrett's soft voice did nothing to calm her down.

She launched her body at Jeremy. Fists pummeled his chest as she called him names and battered his arms and shoulders. He held her and shifted his head to keep from being punched in the face, but otherwise didn't defend himself.

He ached for her. Anything she needed to do to wipe out the pain, he'd accept.

"Meredith, that's enough." Sara laid a gentle hand on Meredith's back and the pounding stopped. "It's okay."

Sara shot Jeremy a murderous scowl as she soothed her new friend. Helplessness like Jeremy had never known pulled him in every direction. The joy at solving the case crashed under the weight of seeing a strong woman brought to her knees.

Meredith pulled up straight and pushed her shoulders back. She looked at Sara and no one else. "You were right. Falling for them will kill you."

And she walked out of the room.

"What just happened?" Jeremy whispered in stunned silence.

Joel and Ellis made excuses to leave the room. Garrett frowned. Sara lost it.

She pointed out the open doorway. "Go apologize."

"I couldn't tell her and keep her safe." Jeremy repeated the mantra playing in his head.

He'd done it for her own good. He'd wanted her as far removed from the lies and deception as possible. Yet somehow he'd dropped her right in it.

"You could, but you chose not to." Sara added Garrett to her glare zone.

He held up his hands in surrender. "Don't look at me. I told you the truth."

"Why?"

Garrett didn't hesitate. "Because I love you."

The comment had Sara smiling. "I know."

Garrett raised an eyebrow in response but didn't say anything.

The scene confused the crap out of Jeremy. Yeah, he knew Sara was the right woman for his brother. Jeremy had always known, but Garrett had always been so tight-lipped about his feelings for her. He acted as if she was just the one who'd landed on his doorstep when he was ready to settle down. Convenient, but not as important as she should be.

He'd put Sara to the side and focused on his job, then joined her when the work was done. But that wall had crumbled. The way Garrett looked at Sara now was so intimate that Jeremy started to squirm. Maybe some things weren't his business.

"And we'll have a wedding. A real one, with a dress and flowers and whatever else you want." Garrett's good mood slipped. "Just don't make me plan it."

Sara's smile grew wide enough to light up the room.

Jeremy wanted to be happy for them but he was too busy wallowing. "What is going on here? We're talking about Meredith."

Garrett exhaled. "No, man. We're talking about you."

"What does that mean?"

"I've been there. I pushed Sara away because I was so scared about losing her. It's illogical but normal for what we do." Garrett clapped a hand against Jeremy's back. "Don't make my mistakes. Don't waste time."

The lecture made sense for Garrett but not for Jeremy. He'd always been the easygoing one. "But I'm not like you...."

Or was he?

Life raced along for him at a steady pace. He took risks and didn't shun commitment. Then a woman had died in front of him, leaving blood on his hands, and something in his mind clicked. Keep a solid distance. Don't get involved.

His mind flashed to Meredith. The pain digging in his chest had him rubbing space to try to ease the pain. But his mind kept spinning. To the woman rolling around in bed with him. To the devastated one in the hospital room.

He had to find her.

He tried to push Garrett but his big brother stopped him. "Where are you going?"

Jeremy dropped his guard and let them see the emotions fighting inside him. "To beg if I have to."

Sara smiled. "It's about time."

## Chapter Twenty-One

Meredith stood at the side of her hospital bed and pressed her hands against her stomach to keep from heaving. Her muscles ached and her hands shook. Reaction to the danger and the fallout had her body in a vise grip and it kept tightening.

She knew her response to being blocked by Jeremy, to all that had happened, flew well out of bounds. Seeing them all standing around laughing while she prayed for him to come out of a fake coma made her the dumbest woman alive. Even at her lowest point during her relationship with Clint, she'd never felt as pathetic as she did right then.

Despite all that, the truth was, Jeremy didn't owe her anything. He'd never made any promises. Not cluing her in to his plan hurt her as much as being banged around in that SUV as it almost went off the cliff, but his work was his work and she didn't belong in the middle of it.

But thinking he was hurt or, worse, dead, sucked the life right out of her. Her brain burned from the pain. She'd been willing to humiliate herself and sacrifice Sara in front of the doctor and everyone else if it meant helping Jeremy.

And it had all been a big joke. On her.

She grabbed the T-shirt she'd worn there and reached

for the hem of the scrubs. She got the shirt halfway up her stomach when Jeremy's deep voice stopped her.

"I'm happy to watch a striptease, but you should know I'm standing here."

She spun around. "What are you doing in my room?"

"Apologizing."

*No, no, no.* She was on the verge of breaking down. Seeing him ate away at her.

She held up her hands as if to fight off the words. If he tried to give her the same lame excuse he'd offer to an insignificant coworker, she would melt into a puddle. He'd reduced her to that.

Falling for him was killing her.

"It's fine. Go celebrate with your friends." She turned her back on him and opened her mouth to draw in huge sweeping breaths.

The tactic didn't work. The panting wouldn't stop and all of a sudden his handsome face appeared in front of her.

Sadness tugged at the corners of his eyes. "I want to be with you."

This was about the sex. Had to be.

Gathering all her energy, she forced her voice to stay steady. "Look, you showed a girl a good time but it's time for me to go."

"Stop."

His hands moved to her shoulders and her body jolted. She had to stay stiff to keep from curling into him. Her strength waned and her head spun. She couldn't take much more.

"It needs to be said." She tried to shrug out of his hold but his grip stayed firm.

"The distance thing doesn't work on you."

It was the wrong thing to say. Her temper flared out of control. This time when she pulled her arms back he let go. "And just what do you know about me? You let me ride around with you and get shot at. We had sex. It meant nothing."

He didn't try to touch her again. His arms hung loose at his sides. "Everything."

Her fury crashed into a pile inside her. "What?"

"It meant everything and I was an idiot not to include you in the plan." He raised his hand again. This time his fingers slipped into her hair. "I kept telling myself that you had seen enough violence in your life and that I had to stop adding more."

The combination of his hands and the closeness of his mouth wrecked her concentration. "So you pretended to be dead?"

"In my stupid male brain it made sense."

She put her hand over his where it rested on her cheek. "Jeremy, I—"

He framed her face in his hands. "You told me I was flawed. That was the understatement of the year. My mind is a mess over the Serena mistakes. The guilt eats at me."

"It wasn't your fault."

"But hurting you was."

She wanted to argue but couldn't. He put her in this place where she doubted her feelings and feared the future again. "It's okay. I'm fine."

If being so numb inside she worried she was dead meant fine. Yeah, she was good.

"I'm not." He placed a sweet kiss on her lips. "Without you, I'm lost."

The words kick-started her heart. "But you have your work and your—"

He kissed her again. This one went on and dragged her along with him. When he lifted his head, she saw the hope she felt in her heart mirrored in his eyes.

"Stay with me. Give me a chance to show you how a man should treat a woman. Let me take care of you, walk with you, comfort you."

Each phrase was a vow. She felt the words as he said them. Saw the determination in his eyes and the worry lingering underneath. She finally saw it. He thought she was going to push him away.

But she couldn't believe. Not yet. "I can't live like Sara did. You can't shove me in a corner and forget about me for days and months at a time. I deserve better and so does she, but the real answer is it will kill me to be that disconnected."

Then she stopped talking. Her gaze searched his face for any reaction, knowing her entire future depended on what he said next.

A smile broke across his mouth.

"I'll share with you all that I can about my work and not walk into danger just to prove I can." His thumb rubbed against her bottom lip. "No more undercover work. At night I come home to you. Only you. And, I'm hoping, forever."

A sob broke in her chest. The wall of pain inside her broke free. Falling for him wasn't hard. She wondered if loving him would be.

"Well?" He actually looked nervous.

Or he did until she wrapped her arms around his neck. "You have to do something for me first."

The tension arcing across his shoulders fizzled. He pulled her tight against him with his arms around her waist and his fingertips brushing her bare skin. "Anything."

"I don't have anywhere to live."

"Funny, I was thinking of asking for a transfer to San Diego. With the shooting, and my time in service and record, it shouldn't be an issue." His hand traveled up her bare back. "And I'll need a roommate."

"That's convenient, because so will I." She kissed him with all the saved-up passion that had been brewing inside her. The promise, the possibilities, the future, she could taste it all on his lips.

The seconds ticked by and the heat built between them. When he pulled back she nearly threw him on the bed and told him to lock the door.

"One request," he said against her mouth. "Not Coronado."

She threw her head back and laughed. "I can't afford it anyway. And I'd rather save money for our future."

"Now there's a plan we can work on together."

WITH EACH STEP, his shoes clicked against the linoleum. Bars clanged behind him as doors opened and shut. He blocked the rumble of inmate voices and shouts aimed in his direction. He had one goal—the room at the end of the hall.

The guard put his hand on the handle, waiting for the agreed-upon signal. With a nod, the guard punched in the security code and swiped his card.

The door creaked open but the man inside at the table didn't look up. Word was the man was expecting his lawyer. The new one. When the prosecutor brought charges against the old one as an accessory, the man had turned on Bruce. The judge froze most of Bruce's accounts until the money could be traced and the origin authenticated. Until then, he was stuck with a public defender.

"You're late." Bruce Casden traced a pattern on the table as he spoke.

"Technically, you're not expecting me. Not breathing, anyway."

Bruce slammed his back against his chair and looked up. All the color drained from his face. "Hill."

"Jeremy Hill, to be exact." He didn't bother sitting down. He had no intention of staying that long anyway.

"You're dead."

Jeremy crossed his arms over his chest and leaned against the door. He'd planned this scene for a week. He was ready to relocate to his new place with Meredith in San Diego. That meant the announcement of his sudden reincarnation would hit the newspapers soon.

But Bruce would hear the news from Jeremy. He'd earned that. "As with everything else in your life, you messed that up."

Bruce snarled. Gone was any semblance of humanity. "I can still make it happen."

"Not without money. Not without power."

"You really think you're succeeding in taking both?" Bruce cackled more than laughed.

"I'll ask your free lawyer when he gets here."

"Your death was all over the news."

"Faked for your benefit."

"Your brother—"

"Also fine." Jeremy smiled as Bruce's face turned even whiter. The man knew what that meant. All his careful planning had gotten him was a stack of new charges and the prosecutor's office was filing them now. "You failed from every angle."

"This time."

"Every time. That's what I came to tell you." Jeremy pushed off the wall and leaned over the desk across from Bruce. "You had your one shot at me and blew it. I'm willing to forget it. You rot in prison and I never see you again. That's the deal."

Bruce shook his head. "I'm going to get out of here."

"No, you're not."

"Then why are you so afraid?"

"I'm letting you know I'm not going to kill you over Serena."

"That stupid bi—"

Jeremy grabbed Bruce by the throat and shoved him until his head hit the wall. Bruce kicked and gagged. The temptation to squeeze just a bit harder and end this thing nearly overwhelmed Jeremy.

He remembered the life he wanted with Meredith and eased up on his grip. "You are going to leave me alone. Me and my brother and everyone I know."

Bruce grabbed at Jeremy's hands but couldn't peel them off. "Why should I?"

"Because if you don't, I'll kill you. You know me, Bruce. You know I will do it."

"You don't scare me."

"I should. I've been itching to take you down for Serena. But I have better things to do these days. You spending the rest of your life in prison is enough, but only barely." Jeremy let go.

Bruce whooshed to the floor in a coughing fit. "No deal."

"Just remember I have the power of Border Patrol and the DIA behind me. That's a whole bunch of people who know how to make scum like you disappear."

Bruce continued to hold his neck. "You follow the rules. There's no way."

"Everyone has a line. You found mine. I suggest you not try to cross it again." Jeremy headed for the door. "We're done talking."

"I'm not."

But Jeremy kept going. Bruce's shouts bounced off the walls as Jeremy walked down the hall.

He kept going, through gates and checkpoints, until he hit the main door and walked out into the bright day. The heat hit his face and he closed his eyes to enjoy it. When he opened them again, a car sat at the end of the long yard on the other side of the gate.

Meredith leaned against the side of the car looking like a mix of sunshine and sex. Her dress reached her knees but the thin straps showed off her shoulders. Either way, he'd have her out of it soon.

She was the woman who restarted his life. The one who made everything right and washed away the darkness.

"Hey, sailor." She wound her arms around his neck and gave him a quick kiss as soon as she reached her.

He rubbed his hands up and down her back, loving the feel of her. Loving every part of her. "I'll have you know we're an army family."

"I don't care what you are so long as we can go home." *Home.*

With her he'd found that. "I'll go anywhere with you."

"Then lead the way."

\* \* \* \* \*

# REQUEST YOUR FREE BOOKS!
## 2 FREE NOVELS PLUS 2 FREE GIFTS!

**◆ Harlequin**

# INTRIGUE

## BREATHTAKING ROMANTIC SUSPENSE

**YES!** Please send me 2 FREE Harlequin Intrigue® novels and my 2 FREE gifts (gifts are worth about $10). After receiving them, if I don't wish to receive any more books, I can return the shipping statement marked "cancel." If I don't cancel, I will receive 6 brand-new novels every month and be billed just $4.49 per book in the U.S. or $5.24 per book in Canada. That's a saving of at least 14% off the cover price! It's quite a bargain! Shipping and handling is just 50¢ per book in the U.S. and 75¢ per book in Canada.* I understand that accepting the 2 free books and gifts places me under no obligation to buy anything. I can always return a shipment and cancel at any time. Even if I never buy another book, the two free books and gifts are mine to keep forever.

182/382 HDN FEQ2

Name _____ (PLEASE PRINT) _____

Address _____ Apt. # _____

City _____ State/Prov. _____ Zip/Postal Code _____

Signature (if under 18, a parent or guardian must sign)

Mail to the **Reader Service:**
**IN U.S.A.:** P.O. Box 1867, Buffalo, NY 14240-1867
**IN CANADA:** P.O. Box 609, Fort Erie, Ontario L2A 5X3

Not valid for current subscribers to Harlequin Intrigue books.

**Are you a subscriber to Harlequin Intrigue books
and want to receive the larger-print edition?
Call 1-800-873-8635 or visit www.ReaderService.com.**

* Terms and prices subject to change without notice. Prices do not include applicable taxes. Sales tax applicable in N.Y. Canadian residents will be charged applicable taxes. Offer not valid in Quebec. This offer is limited to one order per household. All orders subject to credit approval. Credit or debit balances in a customer's account(s) may be offset by any other outstanding balance owed by or to the customer. Please allow 4 to 6 weeks for delivery. Offer available while quantities last.

**Your Privacy**—The Reader Service is committed to protecting your privacy. Our Privacy Policy is available online at www.ReaderService.com or upon request from the Reader Service.

We make a portion of our mailing list available to reputable third parties that offer products we believe may interest you. If you prefer that we not exchange your name with third parties, or if you wish to clarify or modify your communication preferences, please visit us at www.ReaderService.com/consumerschoice or write to us at Reader Service Preference Service, P.O. Box 9062, Buffalo, NY 14269. Include your complete name and address.

HI11B

SO YOU THINK YOU CAN WRITE

Harlequin and Mills & Boon are joining forces in a global search for new authors.

In September 2012 we're launching our biggest contest yet—with the prize of being published by the world's leader in romance fiction!

Look for more information on our website, **www.soyouthinkyoucanwrite.com**

So you think you can write? Show us!

*In the newest continuity series from Harlequin®
Romantic Suspense, the worlds of the Coltons and their
Amish neighbors collide—with dramatic results.*

*Take a sneak peek at the first book, COLTON DESTINY
by Justine Davis, available September 2012.*

"**I**'m here to try and find your sister."

"I know this. But don't assume this will automatically ensure trust from all of us."

He was antagonizing her. Purposely.

Caleb realized it with a little jolt. While it was difficult for anyone in the community to turn to outsiders for help, they had all reluctantly agreed this was beyond their scope and that they would cooperate.

Including—in fact, especially—him.

"Then I will find these girls without your help," she said, sounding fierce.

Caleb appreciated her determination. He *wanted* that kind of determination in the search for Hannah. He attempted a fresh start.

"It is difficult for us—"

"What's difficult for me is to understand why anyone wouldn't pull out all the stops to save a child whose life could be in danger."

Caleb wasn't used to being interrupted. Annie would never have dreamed of it. But this woman was clearly nothing like his sweet, retiring Annie. She was sharp, forceful and very intense.

"I grew up just a couple of miles from here," she said. "And I always had the idea the Amish loved their kids just as we did."

"Of course we do."

"And yet you'll throw roadblocks in the way of the people best equipped to find your missing children?"

Caleb studied her for a long, silent moment. "You are very angry," he said.

"Of course I am."

"Anger is an…unproductive emotion."

She stared at him in turn then. "Oh, it can be very productive. Perhaps you could use a little."

"It is not our way."

"Is it your way to stand here and argue with me when your sister is among the missing?"

Caleb gave himself an internal shake. Despite her abrasiveness—well, when compared to Annie, anyway—he could not argue with her last point. And he wasn't at all sure why he'd found himself sparring with this woman. She was an Englishwoman, and what they said or did mattered nothing to him.

Except it had to matter now. For Hannah's sake.

*Don't miss any of the books in this exciting
new miniseries from Harlequin® Romantic Suspense,
starting in September 2012 and running
through December 2012.*